Contents 3

Dedication 5

Author's Note: 7

Prologue 11

~ 1 ~ 19

~ 2 ~ 33

~ 3 ~ 47

~ 4 ~ 55

~ 5 ~ 67

~ 6 ~ 81

~ 7 ~ 91

~ 8 ~ 101

~ 9 ~ 109

~ 10 ~ 117

~ 11 ~ 127

~ 12 ~	143
~ 13 ~	157
~ 14 ~	171
~ 15 ~	183
~ 16 ~	195
~ 17 ~	209
~ 18 ~	229
~ 19 ~	247
~ Epilogue ~	263

Refined Silver

Dedication

I dedicate this book first and foremost to God, Christ, and the Holy Spirit who searched for me, rescued me, and broke the chains of generational curses so that my children may forever live outside of those cycles. Thank you for saving me and offering the greatest gift, salvation and redemption through Christ, in which all hope is found! To my best friend and the greatest man I have ever known on this earth, my husband (C.L), for loving and honoring me in all ways, for leading our family in such a godly way, for being my best friend who always supports me, for being my protector, the only one to calm the raging seas inside of me. Thank you for seeing all of me instead of just the broken pieces of me, thank you... for choosing me. Still and forever, D4W. To my 4 amazing children (Z.L ., H.L. ,M.L., K.L.), through y'all I have learned what true love is! I am so proud of each of you, and I thank God daily that I get to be your mom! Being your mom and the wife to your dad will always be my greatest purpose; y'all are my entire world and all that is good in it! Y'all are my sunshine, and I will always love you to the moon and back! To my best friends and mentors:

C.D., S.N., S.J., S.O.M staff, thank you for supporting me, holding me accountable, teaching me, strengthening my walk with Christ, and always being my tribe! I am the woman and disciple I am because of your influence, guidance, and love, and I hope to be even half of who you are. To my Mom & Dad and Ma & Pa, thank you for adopting an orphan girl into your family, thank you for loving me and being the family I never had, it is an honor to be your daughter! Last but not least, to J.R. for giving me the platform to help others and for all your hard work creating and publishing this book. You are an answer to our prayers, and it is an honor to work with you and know you. Thank you for having a servant heart, immense wisdom, and the best humor. Any ripple of hope, triumph, or redemption that may happen in helping others see God's love during their darkness is because of the ripple effect all of y'all have had on me. I love you all!

Refined Silver

Author's Note:

When God called me into ministry, I had a Moses moment, questioning if someone else would be better for what he called me to do. You see, I'm more of a Peter than a Paul I'm a lot. I've been told I'm a lot my whole life. I have a lot boldness, a lot of strength, a lot of truth, a lot of mouth, but also a lot of heart. My whole life, I've been "too much." (Shout-out to all of those who always had report cards that said you talked "too much"). When you're "too much," it can be intimidating to others. It's often a lonely road filled with small rooms incapable of containing your big spirit.

When you have "too much" heart, it gets broken often, or you get foot-and-mouth disease, where good intentions lead you to insert your foot into your mouth without even thinking. When you're told you're "too intimidating," a word that literally means to frighten or overawe, it can cause you to dim your light to prevent your loud spirit from triggering others' insecurities, or worse….being misunderstood. No matter how kind I am, how outgoing, forgiving, or welcoming I am, my strong spirit is always "too much" for others.

So, I thought I was "too much" for ministry, "too much" for God's purpose. Putting my loud spirit on display and exposing the darkest parts of my life was something I never wanted to do, but God had greater plans than my insecurities and loud spirit tried to extinguish. I've been through hell, and by God's grace, I have walked out of the flames refined. Now God has called me to carry buckets of water to help those still consumed by the fire. To remind others who have been through trauma or difficult times in their lives that the same God of Abraham, David, and ancient Israel.... is eternal and is the same God of today! He is limitless, full of grace and mercy, and he loves you and is always with you. His light has shown the brightest during the darkest parts of my life; he has never left me or forsaken me even on my worst days, and Christ's grace is ALWAYS sufficient.

This book may be "too much" for some; it may be triggering as you read my fictional non-fiction biography (names of people have been changed to protect others' identities *cue Law and Order opening song*). It contains sexual assault, domestic violence, drug abuse, and mental illness. It is raw and messy, as the depravity of man is raw and messy, but it is full of Christ's triumph and restoration of my life. As you read my story, you may be instinctively sad or angry. However, I hope you see God's faithfulness, Christ pouring out mercy and grace upon me, and the Holy

Spirit supernaturally interceding and sanctifying me so that I may reflect the image of Christ.

I pray you see hope instead of despair, courage instead of fear, and forgiveness instead of resentment. Redemption instead of imprisonment, love instead of hate, and in every instance…God's merciful grace and goodness! I hope you see that God is for you! He is the ultimate healer, comforter, friend, and father, and there is beauty in the darkness!

> Malachi 3:3 says: 'He will sit as a refiner and purifier of silver.'

This verse puzzled some women in a Bible study and they wondered what this statement meant about the character and nature of God.

One of the women offered to find out the process of refining silver and get back to the group at their next Bible study.

That week, the woman called a silversmith and made an appointment to watch him at work. She didn't mention anything about the reason for her interest beyond her curiosity about the process of refining Silver.

As she watched the silversmith, he held a piece of silver over the fire and let it heat up. He explained that in

Refined Silver

refining silver, one needed to hold the silver in the middle of the fire where the flames were hottest as to burn away all the impurities.

The woman thought about God holding us in such a hot spot; then she thought again about the verse that says: "He sits as a refiner and purifier of silver."

She asked the silversmith if it was true that he had to sit there in front of the fire the whole time.

The man answered that yes, he not only had to sit there holding the silver, but he had to keep his eyes on the silver the entire time it was in the fire. If the silver was left a moment too long in the flames, it would be destroyed.

The woman was silent for a moment. Then she asked the silversmith, "How do you know when the silver is fully refined?"

He smiled at her and answered, "Oh, that's easy — when I see my image in it."

-Author Unknown

Prologue

My life is a story written by God's grace. I don't know the ending or how many plot twists remain. But, man, what a page-turner it has been so far, and the beauty of it all is that it's just getting started!

Have you ever wondered how someone can be kindhearted while talking of throat punching people? How is it that a sometimes pink, blue, purple- haired, sassy-mouthed woman with tattoos loves God, Jesus, and the Holy Spirit, speaks of fairy tales, unicorns, and rainbows, yet is born out of evil and despair? How an orphan meets the most amazing Father!

Like all great stories, it is filled with laughter, strength, courage, love, and a whole lot of God's grace!

As legends have told us, a story of a Valkyrie should start at the beginning, and since this is the story of a great heroine, that's where we will begin.

I don't remember the day I was born, but I expected it to be was something like this.

Refined Silver

Once upon a time, on a hot summer night in the South, lightning lit up the sky as if God's angels were playing a symphony of colors and light, rain drops paused in mid air, and a sudden loud roar of thunder shakes the earth like a lion in the clouds, when a red-haired little girl named Brandy was born.

Meteorologists will claim this event was just a typical summer storm, and my family will say it was my angels crying because they were just assigned to the hardest person yet. But this is my story, and I can tell it however I want, and I want to be born a Valkyrie.

In reality, looking back on the day I was born, it should have been an indication of the years laying ahead. The true story is that my father was an abusive alcoholic, and my manic-depressed bipolar mother was addicted to drugs and the wrong kind of man. The night I was born, my father lay drunk and passed out in the hall while his rights were read to him, as he had been arrested for DUI after my maternal grandmother called the police on him. All the while my mother lay in the bed screaming for his freedom. Jerry Springer, here we come! I was named after the alcohol that was coursing through his veins on the night his first daughter was born.

Refined Silver

Brandy the drink and Brandy the most magically awesome heroine (that's me, in case you missed that part) share more than just a namesake. Brandy is a strong spirit whose name translates to "burnt wine." Brandy is made from applying heat and fire to wine or fruits that have sugar. After open flames are applied, it drives out water, leaving only alcohol. The process starts all over and is applied several times, each time going through cycles of fire and heat as the process refines the content until it is ready to go through the aging process. Aging consists of letting it ferment in a dark, cold place before it comes out as a strong drink with notes of sweetness, flowers, and a little zest that is favored all over the world.

It's similar to refining silver. The silver is placed in the middle of the hottest part of the fire to melt off impurities, constantly under the silversmith's watchful eye to ensure that the silver is purified and not damaged. He knows it is purified and finished when he sees his image in the silver.

This book is a testimony of God refining me, putting me in the fire to melt away the impurities, and living out the image of God, Jesus, and the Holy Spirit. While I may not actually be a Valkyrie, I am a child of God and a royal heiress to the Kingdom. I have been to hell and back, and now God has called me to carry watering buckets to help put out the flames of hell in others' lives and remind them of God's goodness even in the midst of the fire.

The first 4 years of my life are little snapshots in my head rather than reels of moments. I remember a snapshot of being in foster care with my two younger sisters because we were found on the riverbank alone in the winter. Another snapshot of finding out on a supervised visit that my mother (we shall call her Spice) was pregnant again and I was going to have a baby brother. Another snapshot of us children being dropped off at a trailer of some man who always had candy and snack cakes for us as we waited for what seemed like forever for Spice to come in from the tobacco fields.

I'm sure I had years of laughter, moments of grit, make-believe and girly things, but I can't recall a single snapshot in my mind of a joyful moment during those first 4 years. Maybe I had lots of joy and I just don't remember, but I have a gut feeling that probably isn't the reality.

My very first memory is in the Pre-K era around 4-5 years old. I got off of the bus that warm afternoon and can feel the sun warm my skin like the warmest of hugs. I remember it making me so warm and tingly that even now I can feel the comforting heat deep down in my soul. I'm standing there in the driveway with my eyes closed and my hair blowing in the wind like I'm flying by the sun on a destination to meet this magnificent presence up high in the sky. I don't know what or who or where it is, but I just know in my heart that it's the most wonderful place, and it gave me a marvelous peace in my heart. Suddenly, I hear my siblings' crying and screaming coming from inside the house.

I don't recall my parents fighting before this, but they must have done so frequently, because I am immediately overcome with fear and knowledge that they are fighting again, but this time seems different. It was as though the air suddenly turns colder and the wind rattles my bones, like the world is emulating the emotions that are raging inside the house. I go into the house, and my siblings are in the back bedroom bawling and screaming in fear; the sheer panic on their faces is forever seared in my mind; my parents are in their bedroom screaming and I hear the sounds of objects breaking. I tell my sisters to get in the closet and I'll be there in just a minute as I walk into my parents' room and my father (we shall call him Goliath) is lying in the bed in a drunken stupor while Spice is throwing things at him.

Suddenly a marble ashtray is thrown at the ceiling fan, and glass, marble, and wood come crashing down, slicing his leg. He jumps out of bed and hits her over and over until she slides down the wall. Blood is pouring from his leg and her face; somehow it has splattered all over the bed and walls. Mixed in with broken glass and strewn objects, the room resembles a Hollywood horror flick. My baby brother starts wailing, and I rush down the hall to him, grab him, his bottle, and my younger sisters. We hide in the closet as I rock him, trying to calm him while comforting my younger sisters. I whisper fairy tales to them and lightly sing "You are my Sunshine" to distract them. In hopes of erasing all they have seen and heard and overpower the pounding of my heart that I can hear beating in my ears. We sat in that closet for what seemed like hours, as I lay curled around them, watching them as they sleep quietly while I stood guard.

The next day hope is revived as my maternal grandmother (we shall call her Emily) arrives and whisks us off to another state where bluegrass grows and promises of a better life await. Unbeknownst to me at the time, the fire was only getting hotter. Starting a new school is hard enough, but starting a new school impoverished is where grit is made. All the girls had beautiful braided hair and perfect teeth, but I had cavities covering most of my teeth and my hair was teased like the miniature version of Whitesnake meets Joe Dirt.

I'm pretty positive all the hairspray used on my bangs alone, contributed to the ozone layer crisis. I may still have multiple layers covering my scalp after all these years. I bet us 80s kids could walk through a tsunami and our head would still be dry to this day. Kids today have heat-curlers and organic products, we had a high heat curling iron, Aqua-Net and a teasing comb. Our mantra being "The higher the hair, the closest to Jesus."

I digress. For a few months, everything was glorious. I would come home from school and play on the tire swing, watch the cattle graze in the field across from us, and consume Slush Puppies like it was manna from the sky. By far it was the most nostalgic treat from my childhood. The mom and pop store at the end of my grandparents' road had slush puppies and the big life-size cut-out of the White Dog that made sure every time we passed it that I would remember they sold the essence of Unicorn Souls in a cup. Just like the IRS or having to pee when you just get comfortable, I ALWAYS asked for the magical drink every single time we left the house and I got one every time. I know you are asking yourself the most in depth burning question....Yes, of course I mixed the flavors!!!!! 1 pump cherry, 2 pumps blueberry and 80 pumps watermelon because life is short and I have always been one to be extra.

Refined Silver

The light shines in the darkness,
and the darkness has not overcome it.
John 1:5

~ 1 ~

So, by this point, my biological parents have divorced, and I'm a country bumpkin living in the bluegrass state. Ummmm, let me let you in on a little secret... the grass is green... I know, I was disappointed too. I digress. We were living up the road from my Nanny Emily, and as her favorite person, it meant life on easy street, or so I thought.

Spice had managed to find another man just like Goliath. We shall call him Renegade. Just like Goliath, he loved to party and beat on women and children, so the move from North Carolina to Kentucky wasn't really a salvation as much as just a change of scenery. Spice rented an old fashioned, floor creaking, wood furnace in the middle of the room house that sat behind an old mom and pop store The house sat on the hill behind Old Man Bryson's store. A mom-and-pop gas station, grocery store, and pharmacy, all in one small white brick-and-mortar store. The kind of store where very few things ever changed. You could still get "dime candy." (For those of you who may not know, "dime candy" was small individual pieces of candy, such as bubble gum or horehound candy, for 10 cents hence the name "dime candy".) Where they still pumped your gas and had a running tab of credit for everyone who lived in our small-town community.

Best of all, they sold Squeezits!! Like all kids in the 90s, I was obsessed with the sugary fruity drinks that came in plastic squeezable bottles with their own character etched into the plastic. Snow White wasn't the only one with her gang of dwarfs, Squeezits had 7 dwarfs too! Mean Green Puncher, Chucklin' Cherry, Smarty Arty Orange, Berry B. Wild, Silly Billy Strawberry, Grumpy Grape, and the best for last, Rockin' Red Puncher.

This magical drink led me to receive the greatest of whoopin's I ever received. One drop of the sweet goodness made it worth every belt lick. Spice was at work, and I had convinced our babysitter that the $30 of loose change and bills that sat atop our TV was so I could buy treats at Old Man Bryson's store. I took the money and unregretably purchased every 6-pack flavor of Squeezits, and then spent the evening with my siblings and I consume every bottle before Spice arrived home. Every time we went into the store, we would beg Spice to buy us a pack , but she never would buy them because she said they were too expensive. They had just released the new addition, magic pellets, and I just had to try the magic in a plastic bottle fruit drink. I know what you're thinking: what are these magic pellets you speak of? Well, they were little, tiny pellets that fit just right into the tiny opening at the top of the bottle. Once you dropped them into your drink, it magically changed colors before your very eyes as though David Copperfield was performing a show in your living room. I didn't have enough money to buy all 7 packs so what did my heathen self do? I added the 7th pack to Spice's running tab, of course. It never dawned on me that she would find out I charged them to her account or that she might notice all of her money gone. All I could think of was getting to try these enticing drinks.

My siblings and I spent the evening consuming every bottle before Spice arrived home in hopes of hiding the evidence to cover up my crimes. We were so sick from drinking the 48 bottles of pure sugar water, that we threw up all over the house. There was so much thrown up colored liquid, it looked like had slaughtered unicorns all over the house. To make matters worse, come to find out that the money was Spice's money for gas to get back and forth to work every day that week. When she got home and the babysitter told her what happened, I got spanked so hard that I had to sleep on my side for a week due to the soreness of my behind.

My 3 younger siblings and I shared a bedroom and a bed . We shared a twin-size bed that was similar to a hospital bed. You know the kind in the commercials that the head or feet can go up and down with the push of a button? In my 5 year old mind, this was the best bed ever! Because it wasn't just a bed, it was also a torture device meant for me to make my younger sisters and brother scream bloody murder when they were annoying. Anytime they would tattletale, whichever of us siblings that got in trouble would devise a plan for that night. We would wait until the back stabbing sibling fell asleep, then the rest of us would creep off the bed and slowly fold it up until they woke up thinking a boa constrictor had wrapped itself around them. If they screamed, we would close the bed up even more until they would cry uncle, and we would start to unfold the bed. Only to suddenly change our minds and close it up again several more times before finally releasing them from the taco entrapment.

The lack of oxygen from being folded up like a taco may or may not have been the reason they are a little weird today; I neither can confirm nor deny these hilarious and cruel practices took place but if they did, it would be called a "character building exercise."

The bedroom may have been a fun jungle gym, but outside of the house was the scariest nightmare ever in my young mind. The house was beside a graveyard, which I had convinced myself was Satan's headquarters. If you stepped outside at night, his demonic soldiers would recruit you; forever confining you to the tombstone-ridden property. A black haired witch patrolled the grounds from our front porch which was beside our bedroom. Sharing a bed with 3 other people isn't comfortable, but when you're sleeping right beside ghosts and goblins, it's a gift in disguise.

But, it was worth it living next door to the zombie making evil lair , because my Nanny Emily was only a mile and a half away. Which meant home-cooked meals, sweets galore, and dancing in the living room to Chuck Berry's "My Ding A Ling" or The Temptation's "My Girl." Where we would "Roll Down the River" with Tina Turner, "Twist" with Chubby Checkers, or have "Georgia On My Mind" with Ray Charles.

Nighttime was spent in intense games of Scrabble or Rummy where Nanny Emily took no prisoners. Afterwards we would have a late-night sweet treat while we were serenaded by the greats—Elvis, Aretha Franklin, Gladys Knight, or Frank Sinatra—on a soulful vinyl record. Once the needle rode the label, we knew that was our signal it was bedtime.

One late night in the Fall, my siblings and I were asleep in our bed while Renegade and his friends had been partying all night. Suddenly the music stopped, and shouting ensued. The inebriated, high as a kite, adult guests quickly left, leaving me to defend my mother and siblings yet again. I get up and run into the kitchen to see him beating her with a metal pipe from under the sink. At first, I'm screaming for him to stop, but he can't hear me over her screams, not that it would have mattered. All of the screaming has now woken my siblings, and they are screaming and crying as well, which only adds to the hysterics in the house.

During this commotion of everyone screaming out of fear, I notice Spice is no longer screaming....she isn't doing anything. She is laying in a pool of her blood, beaten beyond recognition, eerily limp and still. Gaping wounds are all you on her face, it doesn't even look like a face anymore, just a severely bloodied ball of matted blood hair. Her arms are unnaturally bent in a way that you can tell they are both crushed from trying to block the blows from the pipe. I know at this point I have to get help because I'm sure she is dead. We didn't have a house phone, which meant leaving the house alone and getting to Nanny Emily's as quick as I could.

I quieten the kids as I hide them under the bed/torture machine, then run out the front door and down the road to my Nanny's house. As soon as I make it off the porch, reality sets in... I'm about to be a zombie or haunted spirit in the graveyard because I touched the sacred ground at night. It's so dark, I can't see anything. Is the witch chasing me or, worse, is Renegade following me? What if he is following me and kills me like he did Spice? Who will take care of my siblings? What was I thinking?! I'm afraid of the dark, and I'm running barefoot at 2 a.m. in the country where maybe 7 houses reside on a mile and a half stretch. In the country, there aren't any street lights or city glares; everyone is sleeping by 10 p.m., so lights are off everywhere. It's just dark—the deep dark where it seems like it could absorb any light and snuff it out.

Fear has now riddled my body; the emotion of fear has become all too familiar, but this time was different. I know he has killed her, and I have to hurry to save my siblings. If he finds them, he will kill them too. So I run as hard and as fast as I can, and I pray aloud to God. I beg God to help me as I run, I beg him to help me run. With each stride, my body becomes weaker while the desperation in my voice grows stronger. "Lord, please let her be alive. God, please take away my fear of the darkness and give me courage because I'm so afraid and I have to run." I need to run faster and harder than my 5-year-old self has ever run before. But I can't see my own feet because it's so dark. I can't see where I'm running, so I have to rely on my other senses to guide me. I can only hear them on the pavement and feel the difference in the ground when I run too close to the edge of the road. I'm so cold that my body hurts. I can barely bend my fingers as they have stiffened from exposure to the windy, below-freezing temperatures. If I fail, they all die. "Lord, please don't let me fail. I'm so scared! God, I need you! Please help me!"

Refined Silver

My feet are frozen and numb to the point that they feel as if they are a foreign object, as they are no longer an extension of me. My chest burns from gasping in the cold air as I struggle to continue running. My legs feel feeble and tremble with each stride as though they will desert me at any moment. I'm cold, tired, and scared for my safety and my siblings' safety most of all. What if I don't succeed, or what if he chases after me? Is Spice alive? Are my siblings still alive at this point? I cry out to God. "Please send an angel; give me light, oh Lord, or I can't do this... I'm so afraid. Lord, please hear me."

Suddenly, there is this light that engulfs me. Not like a UFO coming down to experiment on me, but like the light on a crystal-clear full moon night where everything is bright and you can see the dark world clearly. But as I look up to see where this light suddenly appeared from, there was only a sliver of the moon in the sky and very few stars. However, there is an aura of clarity and brightness, a supernatural light that did not simply cut through the darkness, but as if the darkness knelt down to the light. This light would only go about 2 feet in front of and behind me, but it lit my path... it lit my spirit. It wasn't just a lamp for me to be able to see, there was this supernatural comfort to it, like an angel had instantly wrapped his arms around me and I was in the protection of light, sent from God's own hand. I no longer felt afraid or scared; I wasn't cold any longer or fatigued. I felt at peace and loved more than my heart could ever imagine, to the point where it almost hurt thinking about how loved I felt.

I had this undeniable clarity in the deepest part of my soul that this was God sending me help. So, I just kept running and saying, "Thank you God, please keep me in the light." The coldness from the crisp fall air was gone, and the sting in my chest from crying and running in the cool night disappeared. My body felt restored and better than the one that originally existed. It felt as though I were running to a place that I never knew but somehow always knew was home ... as though I were running towards God and not simply a phone.

Then I hear dogs up ahead; the sounds of their ferocious barking snap me out of the blissful state. The mean old junkyard dogs that chase everything, including cars as they run out into the road and bite the tires, are up ahead. I know I've run a mile, and I'm almost there when the realization and fear hits me hard. These monstrous dogs go after cars and school buses. They are going to kill me, as I am no match for them. But I have to get help; they are counting on me; lives literally hanging in the balance of my hands — my small frozen hands.

I start crying again and beg God to save me so I can save my family... Lord, how can I possibly fight two dogs? I can't sneak past them. Their eyesight is better than mine.

There is no way to go around them. What am I going to do? God, why did you bring me this far for me to fail?! I hear this voice in the depths of my soul telling me that I am his child and am safe, that I should not be afraid, and that I can trust in him.

Suddenly, there is a car right behind me, and they stop to ask me what's wrong. As they roll down the window, I see it's Mrs. Connie, a friend of the family and the same gullible babysitter I had convinced to let me buy Squeezits. The likelihood of any car, let alone one I knew, on the cold, desolate road at 2 a.m. in a place where everything closes and the world sleeps by 10 p.m. was from God...and God alone.

I try to tell her that I have to get to Nanny Emily's house and call the police, because Renegade has killed Spice. I ramble about the dogs up ahead, and they are going to eat me because the graveyard hasn't turned me into a zombie yet. Thankfully, she is able to decipher what I am saying through my ramblings and tears as she tells me to get in the car, promising that she will take me to Nanny Emily's house. I jump in the warm car as the toasty air stings my frozen skin. Within a few seconds on the road, here come the junkyard dogs barking, growling, and biting at the car tires as we pass them safely in the car.

Refined Silver

I make it to Nanny Emily's in a few short moments. I jump out before the car is even in park, and I race up the porch and proceed to bang on the door, screaming and pleading for them to quickly answer the door. No sooner than she opens the door, I collapse on the floor from mental and physical exhaustion. I'm bawling as I tell her what has happened, as she is desperately trying to decipher my words through the tears. She screams for me to slow down and tell her what is wrong. I finally catch my breath just long enough to say Renegade killed Spice before falling into hysterics again. She immediately calls the police and sends Papaw Joe (armed with his gun) to our house to get my siblings. Spice did survive, but was beaten within an inch of her life. She spent the next several weeks in the hospital, practically in a full-body cast.

Now, when I look back on that night, I don't feel fear or sadness as much; instead, I feel such warmth and peace because I know beyond a shadow of doubt that I have felt God's presence. I heard him speak to my soul, and I basked in the glory and the goodness of his light. He was with me every step of the way, even when I doubted him; his love for me was unconditional and was the true salvation I needed. I don't see sorrow or fear, but peace and love from my heavenly father.

He gave me warmth that penetrated to my soul, as though I had sat on my father's lap, embraced with the warmest hug. I can't explain exactly what the light was, but I do know what it wasn't. It wasn't my eyes adjusting to the dark, I had already been on the road for a while. Between where I lived and where the horrible junk yard dogs was roughly a mile apart. My eyes had adjusted long before the light, but there wasn't much it could adjust to. It was so dark, I couldn't see my feet. Have you spent the night in the woods late at night on a new moon? It was like that: without external light, nothing could cut through the darkness.

The light wasn't even the most supernatural thing, it was the warmth in my soul. I was at perfect peace; in a snap of a finger, I was no longer scared, cold, tired , anything else other than delight and peace. I was 100% happy and had a peace that passed all understanding. It was a temporary completion, I felt whole. The closest experience that even comes close to being in the same ballpark, is when you hold your newborn baby for the first time. That feeling you get, where your heart is so full, and your life is so complete, it is as though the world has faded away and all you feel is complete bliss. If you took that and multiplied it by 50, it might come close to the peace I felt.

Even though I could see from the car's headlights , I knew instantly the moment the light vanished. The loss of the light was heartbreaking, and I felt devastated. The cold was so ever-present that my skin stung from the temperature shifts from outside to inside of her car. With the warmth and the light gone, I felt empty compared to just mere moments before. As though I were a hollow shell compared to who I was in the light. My heart was sad and my soul heavy while it ached to be back in the presence of the light. I don't know why or how, but I do know that I was in the presence of God or one of his angels that night. It was the most joyful and pure, "out of this world" feeling that I have ever felt in my life. Christians, at some point in their walk with Christ, may even question if God exist. I can say for certain he does because I have felt his presence and it was the most beautiful experience of my life! If I felt that complete and rejuvenated in my broken sinful body, how glorious will our resurrected bodies be!

Refined Silver

Though I walk in the midst of trouble, you preserve my life. You stretch out your hand against the anger of my foes, with your right hand you save me.

Psalm 138:7

~ 2 ~

While Spice was in the hospital recovering, we spent those 8 weeks with my Nanny and her husband, whom I had only known as my Papaw Joe. Spice's biological father killed himself when she was a young child, and Nanny had remarried a couple of times before settling down with Joe before I was born.

They had a wood furnace in the basement that they used to heat their house in the winter. We would buy a truckload of split wood every fall and stack it in the basement for the winter. The truck of split wood would back up to one of the tiny basement windows, and we would form an assembly line. Someone on the back of the truck would hand the dry logs off to someone on the ground by the window. They would toss it through the window, and someone would be in the basement to grab it and stack it in the corner. I was assigned to the basement position with Joe. Once those outside had finished their positions, they went into the house to warm up while I was still in the basement stacking wood. Before I knew it, Joe grabbed me and forced me onto an old mattress he had in the garage. He lays on top of me to hold me down while he slides my Smurfs jogging pants down. He clamps his hand over my mouth, but really it covers over half of my face due to how large his hand is and how small my face is. He forces his hand inside of me with such immense force that I instantly scream and start crying, but with his hand over my mouth, my screams are muffled and useless. He has sharp nails that feel like they are slicing me with razors each time he slams his hand into me. I am flailing and trying to get away from him, which seems to only add to his arousal. I don't understand what is happening or why it hurts so bad and stings at the same time. I know I have to get away somehow, so I try biting his hand and hitting him repeatedly to no avail. I see the shelves to my left filled with dozens of glass jars of homemade pickles that my grandmother has canned. I try grabbing one to use as a weapon, but they are out of reach no matter how far I try to stretch. My chest is pounding, my hands are shaking, and I'm now struggling to breathe between the hysterical crying and the pressure from his hand over my mouth and inadvertently my nose. He tells me he is going to remove his hand, but if I scream, he will beat me and leave me under the stairs and then sexually assault my younger sisters. He removes his hand as I'm still struggling to get away, and I try bucking him off of me to no avail. I try sliding or crawling away from him, but he is still holding me down while still violating me with his hand, and he isn't budging. He tries to kiss me, but I keep moving my head side to side trying to prevent him from making contact, which leads him to kiss me all over my face with slobbering wet kisses. I try desperately to get away, but the more I try, the more forceful he becomes.

The smell of the mildew in the basement and on the mattress combined with being assaulted makes me so nauseous that I think I may throw up at any moment. He takes my hand and forces it onto his now exposed male part, and he instructs me to grab it and to slide my hand over it while he demonstrates how. After a few minutes, suddenly the basement door opens and we hear one of my siblings start to come down the stairs. He immediately jumps up, and tucks himself back into his pants, as he re-fastens his jeans while screaming for my brother to get back upstairs. During this distraction, I quickly pull my pants up and run past him and upstairs to my nanny.

I dash into the bathroom and pull my pants down to see what's causing this excruciating pain. I'm bleeding, and it stings like when you put sanitizer on your hands and it finds that paper cut you didn't know you had. My legs are shaking so hard, my knees buckle. I try to catch my breath and calm my heart, as it feels like it's beating out of my chest. I can't hold back the nausea any longer and barely make it to the toilet before I throw up. I wash my face with my trembling hands, desperately trying to wash all of his slobber off of me. I keep scrubbing my hands, no matter how much soap I use; they still feel dirty. I scrub them so hard they are fiery red and feel raw. I wish I could cut off my hand, it still feels dirty and gross. I tuck toilet paper into my panties and rush out to find Nanny Emily.

She is at the stove cooking dinner, and I tell her I need to speak to her in private. She puts the lid on the pan and asks me what I need to tell her. I reiterate that it's a secret and we have to talk in private, but before we can go into a different room, Joe comes into the kitchen carrying my baby sister, and we lock eyes. Without even saying a word, his intimidating eyes told me to be quiet and that he would make good on his threat to sexually abuse my sisters like he did me. I tell her never mind, and she returns to cooking as I immediately feel like a coward. I tell my siblings after dinner that they are to never go to the basement ever again. I tell them there is a snake nest down there and that it's too dangerous, in hopes of scaring them away from the basement. I'm too afraid to tell them the real reason in case it gets back to Joe.

Over the next few weeks, Joe always found a way to physically touch me any chance he could, whether it was sneaking up behind and kissing me on the neck. Or forcing me onto his lap at the bar and inappropriately touching me as if it was accidental. I tried to make sure my siblings and I never left my grandmother's side, but he always found a way to touch me.

Once Spice got out of the hospital, I told her what happened, and she made me go and tell Nanny Emily, with Joe sitting beside her, who accused me of lying. She said Spice made me lie to take heat off of Renegade and that she had dropped the charges. I promise her I'm not lying, and she has me go to a sexual abuse investigator therapist to prove I'm telling the truth.

It's hard enough finding the courage to tell Nanny; it's exceptionally harder to tell a stranger. I already felt dirty and worthless, and now I'm in this office showing this stranger what he did to me by demonstrating on a doll. She has me walk through every single detail over and over again. After what dignity I had left was stripped away, they then made me physically strip down for a physical examination. A couple of weeks ago, no one had seen my private parts since I was in diapers. Since then, Joe had sexually assaulted me, so I had to reveal every excruciating detail to a therapist, and now a stranger was elbow-deep in examining my privates. I longed to turn back time and wish it had never happened; I wanted to erase every memory or conversation about it; I wanted it to be over. Joe visits Spice, and they speak in private. After he leaves, she sits me down and tells me to recant and say I lied. If I don't, the state will take us away and separate all of us kids. She tells me Nanny will die of a heart attack, and it will be my fault. Spice says she knows what Joe did to me, but if I don't

Refined Silver

recant, Nanny Emily's death will be my fault and I will never see my siblings again.

I didn't know it at the time, but Joe had paid Spice in an exchange for my silence. She makes me recant to the police and the therapist, but the worst part is that she makes me tell Nanny Emily that I had made it up. Nanny spends over an hour scolding me, telling me that she will never trust me again and that she isn't even sure she wants anything to do with me anymore. Incredibly, Nanny Emily then makes me apologize to Joe. I stand there, unable to even look at him. The man who had sexually assaulted me, who continues to inappropriately touch me…and I tell that I am sorry… ME, not him.

Unbeknownst to us, Spice calls Goliath to come and pick us up, but she tells us it was just for a weekend visit. Spice has me pack a change of clothes for each of us, but we don't have any clean clothes. So, I walk into our little room with our hospital bed and search through the dirty clothes that are scattered all over the floor in hopes to find the least dirty ones for us to take. I shove them in a grocery bag and hug her as I walk out the door. I run back to her for a longer hug as I know deep down something isn't right. I can feel it in my gut. (What I didn't know at the time was that she had called Goliath while in one of her manic depressive states and told him to come get us or she would kill us.)

Refined Silver

Back down to the Appalachian Mountains we go, and for a moment, everything seems to be OK and everyone seems to be outwardly content. Goliath has remarried, and his new wife seems to be able to calm his storms and keep the destruction at bay. It is my fault we are here because I am the one who told the truth and they don't want me anymore. For a very long time, this unnecessary guilt burdened my heart.

One afternoon, Goliath's wife is stressed with one of her grown daughters and takes it out on us. Any time she is stressed or overwhelmed, she makes us deep clean the house. I think partly it's to keep us busy so we aren't making lots of noise playing or creating chaos. My job is to dust the house, and in the process, I accidently knock over one of her porcelain knick-knacks causing it to break into pieces. Before I can even blink, she charges across the room and is in my face, screaming at me. She is so enraged, spittle flies out of her mouth as she is screaming at me, and it lands on my face. I make a mistake and instinctively step back, which only enrages her more. She loses her temper, and her long nails scratch a mole off my neck when she goes to grab my face. I didn't know something so small could bleed for so long. It bleeds pretty heavily all night, and I'm convinced I may bleed to death. Normally, when I'm hit or cut, it bleeds only for a little while and stops, but this time, I continue to bleed no matter how much pressure I apply. I'm going to bleed to death, and this is my punishment for telling the truth, thus sending us back down here.

Goliath's calm nature doesn't last long, as he starts drinking again, which always makes him violent. The next day when he is sober, he apologizes and promises to never drink again. The cycle continues for months and months, and I become an expert at reading people by 6 years old. Picking up on the tones or the tensions in the room becomes a work of art, so much so that it's like I can hear their thoughts and feel their emotions without even an outward appearance from them. I use this gift from God to steer clear of Goliath during his phases or to get my running shoes on so I can run to the neighbors and call the police when staying away is unavoidable. I know to keep the kids quiet when I feel the winds blowing inside of him, to ensure they aren't caught in the devastating effects of the storm. When there is no avoidance, I take the lumps and bumps to spare my siblings the pain and injury. I accept it as another punishment. I am thankful that all I have to endure is physical beatings and not sexual assault. He never ever sexually abuses me, allows any men to come near me, or behaves inappropriately. Sexual abuse is my barometer to measure love. As long as he doesn't sexually abuse me, that must mean he loves me, even if he and his wife hit me.

I am still emotionally healing from all the sexual abuse I suffered back in the Bluegrass State. I still didn't understand why it happened, but it makes me feel dirty and hollow inside. I am fearful and distrusting of all men. So for Goliath to hug me, hold me, and laugh with me without any sexual connotation meant safety, which I desperately long for. Goliath isn't always bad or angry. hen he isn't drinking, he is the greatest father and smartest person I know. But like most alcoholics, Goliath becomes less and less the greatest father, and the drunk and angry one is ever present until that's all that exists. His wife couldn't handle it any longer and leaves us all. She is now the second mother to walk out on us.

I beg Goliath to call Spice. "I'm sure she misses us; please Dad let me call her and hear her voice." He looks me in my eyes, and I can see the bloodshot veins and redness in his. Thunderbird is permeating off his breath so strongly that it seems to cut through the sheer oxygen in the room and fill it with the smell of barley and hops. He tells me she died a few months ago, and I have no mother. The weight of the world comes tumbling down, like the sky itself has fallen. It physically hurts to breathe. I catch my reflection in the mirror on the wall, and I'm a spitting image of Spice. I know Goliath sees it too, as the look of disgust is ever present in his eyes. The turmoil, anger, and pain roll in the depths of his dark brown eyes as though they plead for help, but his soul is held hostage by darkness.

Refined Silver

I think the stress of another broken marriage coupled with alcoholism's firm grip on him has now robbed Goliath of his career, which has led us into poverty, and what money he has is used up in alcohol. It all adds up to the realization that it's our fault, us kids, because if he didn't have 4 mouths to feed and the stress of 4 young children, none of this would have happened. He thinks it's Spice's fault for not being a proper mother and raising her children, thus putting it on him, and here I stand, a mini spitting image of the thing he is angry at the most.

Goliath goes on a week-long drinking binge, one that apparently scares the daylights out of the prostitute he has hired that has now, who has now locked herself in the bathroom, begging for help in the middle of the night. So he comes and wakes me up to go and talk some sense into her. My sleepy 6-year-old self goes and negotiates with her to unlock the door. I hear myself speaking of things as though I have lived a long life with the most experience and advice to offer anyone in that house. It must have only been a few minutes, but it seemed like hours of pleading and negotiating before she finally opened the door. Just enough for him to grab her by her dark curly hair and drag her out of the bathroom and through the house.

Off to the neighbors I go to call for help. We need the police here yet again because I can't talk sense into him when he is raging like this. I don't know if this was the crux of what happened next or if it was the stewing anger found at the bottom of the bottle, but it forever altered my life and desires. The next night, I lay sleeping in the bottom bunk bed of my room, I'm awakened by the knowledge of a presence leaning over me. I can't see what it is—just the shadowy outline—but I quickly realize it's Goliath. I hear a vibrating pop and whistle sound, followed by a sudden immense amount of pain as I hear the cracking sound similar to cracking a chicken quarter. Hot liquid starts gagging me as it fills my throat, but I can't swallow as there is something cold and smooth holding my tongue down. Blood is pouring everywhere and my mind is screaming that I'm in pain, but I just feel numb, like my nerves aren't registering the immense pain in my lower face. He walks away, and I rush out the front door that sits by my bedroom door. I run to the neighbor's house as I struggle to breathe through the large amounts of blood filling my throat. I feel light-headed but the pain in my mind is dulling as I feel weaker and weaker, as though I have become weightless and am fading into the night. As the neighbor opens the door, I see my reflection in the glass screen door.

Blood is pouring down my face, and an arrow is pierced through my bottom lip, which now lies gashed in two and lay bare on my chin. The look of sheer terror on her face is now permanently etched in my mind as I realize this is bad. My brain can't make sense of what I saw in my reflection and what I'm feeling. Why can't I move my tongue? Why is this stick attached to my mouth? Was I dreaming? "Wake up, this is a bad dream, wake up!!"

This is my last thought before waking up in the hospital bed, with people rushing around me in a flurry, but someone is holding my hand. I've never seen him before that I recall, but him holding my hand gives me a comfort that I've never experienced from human contact before, and then I realize it's a police officer. He smiles at me and tells me I'm going to be OK, but his eyes flicker with anger and devastation at the same time. In his eyes, sadness being outweighed by anger is such an oxymoron that it's as if they each have their own emotion and are competing to see which one will win. He is holding a clear bag with a bloody arrow in it as I lay there wondering why he was hunting at night in uniform, and more importantly, why he was holding my hand. Then the realization hits me almost as hard as the arrow. Goliath shot me with his crossbow while I lay sleeping; the reason I couldn't move my tongue was because there was an arrow lodged in my throat. I try to ask him what happened, but I can't speak, and the pain in my throat feels as though it has been rubbed raw by a sander and ripped to shreds. I reach up and feel my face, as it is numb yet still feels three times the size it should be. I feel jagged stitching throughout my bottom lip and halfway down my chin, but when I touch my lip, it sinks in a little. I suddenly have a little dip in my lip. My bottom teeth have been broken down to little nubs, and

Refined Silver

when I press my bottom lip against them, it hurts as the jagged edges of my teeth are rubbing against the stitches. Tears fill my eyes and run down my cheeks. I see the officer come unglued inside as he wipes away my tears and tells me, "You're safe now. I'll stay here with you tonight. I'll keep you safe; he can't hurt you with me here. Get some sleep."

I drifted off to sleep and slept with more peacefulness than I ever experienced to that point, with the realization that for tonight I am safe, and if I make it, I'm going to grow up to be a police officer. I know I want to save people and give them hope when they can't see any. I want to keep people like Goliath and Renegade from hurting any more people. I want to be the hero for the broken. The officer kept his word and sat in the chair beside my bed all night, never letting go of my hand. Several times throughout the night, I would wake for a moment to find him praying for me. Praying for justice and praying for my protection while never dropping his guard to keep me safe... like a warrior from the heavens God sent down to earth. Like usual, Goliath weasels his way out of any trouble, and I go back home with him, but with a new friend. A friend with God on his side as well as a small army of warriors, and I have his number hidden away in my pocket. I have Officer Samson's number. Now I am blessed with a daily reminder, a visual for when I need to see ... a scar to remind me daily of God's power and grace.

Refined Silver

For I was hungry and you gave me something to eat, I was thirsty and you gave me something to drink, I was a stranger and you invited me in, I needed clothes and you clothed me, I was sick and you looked after me, I was in prison and you came to visit me.' "Then the righteous will answer him, 'Lord, when did we see you hungry and feed you, or thirsty and give you something to drink? When did we see you a stranger and invite you in, or needing clothes and clothe you? When did we see you sick or in prison and go to visit you?' "The King will reply, 'Truly I tell you, whatever you did for one of the least of these brothers and sisters of mine, you did for me.'

Matthew 25:35-40

~ 3 ~

After the crossbow incident, things were calm for a while, but the drinking slowly came back, and as the drinking returned, so did the anger and abuse. Yet, the next few years had the most profound impacts on my life and were critical to my walk with Jesus, the joy inside of me, and the woman I became. Saturday mornings Goliath would take us to the store and let us pick out a piece of "dime candy" and he would get his usual Thunderbird or beer and V8 juice, and we would go out to the woods. He would drink himself into a stupor and pass out on the hood of the car while we kids ran free and played as one with nature.

I would take off my shoes and run as fast as I could on the damp forest floor, the wind blowing through my fiery red hair and glinting like the fire yearning to burn in my soul—my first love with Mother Nature and the freedom and calming presence she would bring. Oh how the sun would chase me, like a game of tag, peering through the canopy of the trees, searching for me as the rays broke through and shone on me like a superstar taking center stage. Warmth and joy filling my soul as the warmth of the sun seeped through my skin and deep into my bones. I would close my eyes and listen to the birds singing songs of praise and the insects providing the harmony as though they were praising the heavens, while the sun would radiantly beam with pride.

In those woods, I first learned to drive, which was a blessing as many afternoons when it was time to go, as Goliath would be passed out and I would have to drive us home. My little self scooting to the very edge of the seat so I could reach the pedals while pretending I was an old granny sitting up against the wheel, talking in an old granny voice to keep my siblings calm so I could concentrate. In those woods and on our drive home, our innocence was restored: the day filled with laughter and jokes, hide and seek and treasure hunts; make-believe horse rides on a rickety wire fence that rocked to and fro; climbing trees and swinging on vines like a tire swing. In those woods was sanctity—no fear of anything, just pure bliss and sticky sweetness from our sweet treats. But those Saturdays became fewer and fewer and the bottom of the bottles became deeper and deeper. There were increasing nights of rage because I didn't wash the dishes well enough. Or maybe I burnt dinner or didn't ration it right. There was always a reason why I wasn't good enough and justification for why he would fly in a rage. The smell of alcohol permeating from his breathe so strongly one would think they stood in the middle of a distillery gave way to the real reason. Money became tighter and the availability of food became less and less.

Refined Silver

Hunger is a great motivator, and I soon went door to door on our road asking if I could clean their house or babysit for money. I remember the look on their faces as my tiny 7-year-old self would politely inquire if they were in need of services, as though I could clean a home better than them. A kind family hired me to clean their house twice a week in exchange for groceries, and the lady next door let me babysit her grandchildren when she had to run into town in exchange for $10. That is where I learned hard work and that no job is beneath you if it puts food on the table. Thankfully, school started back, which meant breakfast and lunch, but it also meant I wouldn't be there to get the food stamps out of the mail before he got them. If he got to them before I did, he would trade them for liquor or beer, which meant more hungry nights for us.

I don't know if it was because she knew I would hide part of my breakfast and lunch and take it home every day to give to my younger siblings since they didn't go to school. Or because God put it on her heart, but my Secret Santa started that year and changed the course of my life and education. That year my school had a Halloween/fall festival where every room was decorated with a theme and you were able to play games and win little trinkets like spider rings and pumpkin pencils, but you had to pay for a ticket to enter the carnival and you had to have tickets per activity. We didn't even have money for food, let alone a fun carnival. All the money I was earning went to buy 25-

cent pot pies or beans and rice so we could eat. All week long, all the kids were talking about their excitement and who was going to win bobbing for apples, the costume contest, a pie walk, or go through the haunted house. With each person's excitement, my heart broke a little more, as I would fought back the tears. Friday rolls around, and I'm devastated as I head to the bus for a weekend of cleaning.

The office calls me over the intercom. I walk into the office worried they have found out I have been taking part of my breakfast and lunch home every day and they are going to tell me I couldn't have food anymore. Instead, they hand me a gift bag with an entrance ticket to the carnival, what seemed like an endless supply of tickets, along with a set of cat ears and a tail—attached to a note that said, "Have a Boo-Tastic Time, Love Your Secret Santa."

My spirit warmed me like the sun on those sweet Saturdays as tears of joy rolled down my face. I played every activity that night over and over; I visited every room to the point where I had to have three paper bags to hold all the candy and trinkets I had won. This was also the beginning of my defiant spirit because when I got home, all the candy was placed on the top of the fridge, out of our reach. But every night when I would do the dishes, I would quietly scoot the chair I needed to stand on in order to reach the sink over to the fridge and sneak 4 pieces of candy for my siblings and me to hide and eat later that night.

Refined Silver

From that point on, my heaven-sent Secret Santa would always have a gift bag for me on every holiday, always signed "Love, Your Secret Santa." For Christmas, I would receive a matching sweater and pants, trinkets and chocolate, gloves, and a little Santa. Looking back, I think that was the moment I fell in love with Santa, who today still stirs magic inside of me as hundreds of Santas are scattered throughout my house every Christmas season. Valentine's Day, there would be a heart-shaped box of chocolate; St. Patrick's Day, gold coins and trinkets; Easter was a beautiful Sunday dress and an Easter basket. There was always something for every single holiday, every field trip, and every class party. But the greatest gift she gave me was the gift of food. I never got seconds, because you had to have money and that was something I never had. Day after day I would eat my portion of food and long for more, sometimes trying to convince myself to be selfish and eat my siblings' portion that was squirreled away in my pocket.

One day, I was so hungry to the point I couldn't ignore my hunger pains anymore, and I mustered the courage to go and beg for an extra slice of pizza. I walked up to the lunch lady and ask if there is a burnt piece or a scrap piece that I could possibly have, she beamed from ear to ear and said "Honey, you have money on your account, I was wondering when you were going to use it." She pulled out a white envelope from her drawer with my name and the words Secret Santa written on it, opened it up, and took out one of the dollar bills for my pizza. That second slice of pizza was the greatest thing I have ever eaten. The cheese seemed extra stretchy and the sauce extra sweet. It was like the angels themselves made it and added a touch of magic that seeped into my soul. My Secret Santa had given the lunch lady money to not only cover me getting seconds but also there was enough daily for me to take food home without having to portion my lunch. Every week from that point on, there was an envelope that gave freedom for seconds, for ice cream, or the coveted Slush Puppies on Fridays. Every week, the envelope...of hope arrived. My Secret Santa did this all the way through 5th grade but never revealed herself, only signing, "Love, Your Secret Santa." Then on my last day, I took my report card to every teacher to be signed when my PE teacher, Ms. Pat, signed it. "Love, Your Secret Santa."

I stood there on the gym floor reading it over and over, trying to process that it was her. This can't be! Ms. Pat was always so tough on me. She never let me take it easy and expected more from me than everyone else in class. If we had to run 5 laps, she made me do 6. If I got in trouble on the bus, she would be waiting for me the next day to lecture me and tell me I was better than that. I spent my entire elementary school experience thinking she hated me, when in reality, she was the first adult to unconditionally love me and guide me.

Refined Silver

I run into her arms as she bends down, looking me in the eye and tells me something that sets me on the course of God's plan for me. She told me I was special, more special than anyone she had ever known, and the sky was the limit for me as long as I remembered a few things. "Never ever quit. When you think you can't take another step... run another lap. To believe in myself and push myself beyond what I could imagine. There are two things in this world that you have that no one can ever take from you; these two things will change your life for the better if you pour time and energy into them: knowledge and character. No matter what, no one can ever take away who you are inside—your spirit, your unselfishness, your honesty—that is your character. Absorb as much knowledge as you can because knowledge is power and no one can take that away from you. With these two, you will never be powerless."

For the first time in my life, someone told me I was special, and I knew I never ever wanted to let her down. She was hard on me because she knew I was capable of much more. She was instilling perseverance and determination even when times were tough. She was laying the foundation for my warrior spirit. Still to this day, I absorb knowledge like manna from heaven and am unwavering in my character and who I am as well as the standard I hold myself to...all because of the love of my Secret Santa.

Refined Silver

Finally, be strong in the Lord and in his mighty power. Put on the full armor of God, so that you can take your stand against the devil's schemes. For our struggle is not against flesh and blood, but against the rulers, against the authorities, against the powers of this dark world and against the spiritual forces of evil in the heavenly realms. Therefore put on the full armor of God, so that when the day of evil comes, you may be able to stand your ground, and after you have done everything, to stand. Stand firm then, with the belt of truth buckled around your waist, with the breastplate of righteousness in place, and with your feet fitted with the readiness that comes from the gospel of peace. In addition to all this, take up the shield of faith, with which you can extinguish all the flaming arrows of the evil one. Take the helmet of salvation and the sword of the Spirit, which is the word of God. And pray in the Spirit on all occasions with all kinds of prayers and requests. With this in mind, be alert and always keep on praying for all the Lord's people.

~Ephesians 6:10-18

~ 4 ~

Life with Goliath was the typical cycle of being abused mentally and physically, then having moments of remorse and affirmations of love with the failed declaration of getting sober. Moments of abuse consisted of Goliath pushing my brother through a glass window or the countless broken bones I sustained from the times I tried to intervene and take the brunt of it when he raged on my siblings. Then there would be some days the abuse was not as bad such as a busted nose, spit on or thrown against a wall. Sprinkled throughout were terrifying moments that I questioned my survival, such as the time he stabbed in my ribs with a kitchen knife, cracking my ribs and almost puncturing my lung. Or the time he hit me with a cast iron skillet in the top right side of my head, thus splitting my head open and chipped off a piece my skull leaving a permanent indentation. Another physical reminder of God's goodness. When life is hard and fear wants to set in , I touch my head and feel the sizeable indention where my skill should be; and I'm reminded that God has gracious and has brought me through worse and he will do it again!

Nothing ever changed other than the type or severity of abuse. He didn't just hit or kick; he didn't always wield a weapon or make one out of inanimate objects, what type of abuse you got was unpredictable. What was for certain was that we were alone in this violent world filled with drunken rage, remorse, bribery, and false promises. Rinse and repeat.

The thing about chains of abuse or addiction is that you are unaware of their hold on you; that each day, the same abuse or habit, such as grabbing a drink on a hard day, forms another link in a chain until it has entrapped you so that you are unable to break free. He was chained to the bottle and the disease that had overtaken him as I was being strangled by the chains of domestic violence and child abuse and the effects from it. I would lie in bed at night and see the devil's face smiling at me through the crack in my door, both of us knowing his torture on me would soon begin. People fear the devil for what he can do physically, but the real threat for me was the ability of the enemy to get into my mind and create fear. As I would see him laughing at me, visually I could see myself shrinking smaller and smaller into the size of a tiny fairy. As the door grew, Lucifer grew taller like a scene out of Alice in Wonderland. The larger the door and Lucifer became, the more sheer terror I felt inside. Deep in my soul, I knew the power he could yield and the delight he found in being able to delve into my mind and provoke horrible thoughts and fears. Not from books or movies, but this undeniable awareness that it was pure evil and that evil truly existed.

Refined Silver

I have tried many times since writing this to put into words just how terrifying this was and the emotions that ran through my body. Alas, I have failed because I cannot explain the unexplainable, I know of no words to capture what my soul knew. If the sheer terror and torture I felt just by looking into the face of evil is any indication of the slightest second of hell that exists in the underworld, I will forever spend my life doing everything I can to avoid ever chancing being sentenced to hell, even for a moment. I was afraid of the dark and would spend my nights curled in the corner of my bed, scared of the devil, the monsters in my closet, under my bed, or in the corner, and of course, my father.

I spent hours on watch, constantly scanning the room with my back against the corner so that I could see all angles of the room. I would futilely tell myself the devil can't get me if he can't sneak up on me, as I would try to discern the shapes in the shadows of the dark room. Was that a bunched-up shirt or the devil's minion crouched down waiting for me? I was afraid of the shadows like most children are, but instead of monsters, I feared actual demons. Is something under my bed waiting for the slightest drop in my hand or foot over the side of the bed? I dare not get up to use the restroom or roll away, leaving my back exposed for whatever unsuspecting thing might happen. Nighttime was a war of terror because of the ghastly monsters that formed in my mind and the fear that would make my heart race and my breathing shallow until my little body would pass out from exhaustion. I would pray for hope, for a rescue, or even a sign that it would get better.

As daytime wasn't much better, because of Goliath's descending spiral and tarnished reputation from his drunken stupors, we were deemed undesirables. Poverty-stricken, worthless, dirty, and a blemish in God's creation were how we were treated.

There were two girls that lived on my road, Maddi and Julie Worrell who made my life a living hell , a hell that started at 7:30 every morning. To this day, I don't know why our home life bothered them so much that I had to spend my days being the target of their hatred, but regardless, I was the focus of their discontent. They would be waiting on the bus, armed with quick insults, hair pulling, stealing my backpack, and relentlessly mocking me for being poor, or would ridicule me over the latest antics of Goliath. Going as far as to claim I deserved the bruises or broken bones that I had to carry, for that was proof that even my family didn't want me. Maddi was in my class, while Julie was going into high school, so the insults continued throughout the day and lunch, but with just one, it wasn't as bad. However, the watered-down harassing was just a gear up to the afternoon, where they would be

Refined Silver

together again and would pick apart my self-esteem, word by word.

One day, we had hat day at school, and the only hat I could get was one of Goliath's from his stint at McDonald's for an extremely brief time. I thought it would be fine since everyone loved McDonald's, alas, the sisters did not. They called me Ronald McDonald and would make jokes about me being so poor and ugly that the only thing I could ever do is be the clown for McDonald's, hoping that someone would toss me scraps of food. Each day there were more insults centered around Ronald McDonald and I, months and months of being Ronald McDonald.

One day, we were told to bring in a family recipe as well as the corresponding dish and demonstrate on how to make it, in front of the class. For someone that didn't have food at home, they could have assigned capturing a shooting star and had the same probability on my ability to complete the assignment. I didn't know what to do, but I knew we didn't have food to spare, and if I were caught sneaking any food out of the house, that would be stealing. The beating for breaking a severe rule like stealing would be too severe to risk. I spoke to my teacher and explained that my parents would not allow me to bring food to school, but she just told me I would fail the class if I didn't, and that was that. I thought and thought and finally mustered up the courage to ask the lunch ladies if they had any extra food that I could use for my project. They gave me two heels of bread and a packet of peanut butter and jelly to demonstrate a PB&J sandwich. I was so excited because I knew how to make that, and what kid didn't love a PB&J sandwich? I held my head high and presented it, proud of myself for accomplishing the unattainable. And then I got on the bus that evening to the chants of "Leftover Sandwich," which was the perfect pun since my last name was Leftwich. It also played on the fact that I was poor and had to use leftover bread from the school cafeteria to make a sandwich for my project, while others brought in homemade cakes and lasagnas. It was clever and it was cruel. From that point on, they never called me by name anymore or Ronald McDonald, just "Leftover Sandwich." A mighty blow to my fragile self-esteem, so much so that I would feel defeated every time I stepped off the bus and into the lion's den or onto the bus into the den of snakes. I prayed for God to save me, "Lord, please send me a sign it will be ok. Send me hope, send me an angel."

Jesus sent me, Mrs. Rogers. Mrs. Rogers was the preacher's wife of the church across the road from our house. She looked like Mrs. Doubtfire; and even had similar clothes and a similar purse, she smelled of moth balls and sugar cookies, a combination that was both pungent and welcoming at the same time. I never imagined angels like that; I always envisioned angels as majestic, with long blonde hair and the most pristine and glamorous dress—

one that smelled of the sweetest flower on a dewy spring morning mixed with essences of honeysuckle. One with the most glorious glowing light all around her that radiated from inside her very being. I never thought angels could be in disguise, especially one like Mrs. Doubtfire, but to this day I truly believe God sent me an angel.

My family didn't attend church, but the Bible and God were always present in our home—a convoluted, hypocritical version, but still present none the less. As punishment, we would have to read the Bible and the Encyclopedia collection. At 7-8-years-old, I would read it yet not fully understand, as though I was reading a foreign document where you could only decipher a few words. What I did understand was Goliath could recite every verse in the Bible and would roll out his Jailhouse Religion at the drop of a hat. (You know the sudden faith in Christ when they have gotten in trouble and needs the church and God to get them out of the mess? However, once they are out of the situation, God is no longer uttered from their lips until the next time they get in trouble—that's Jailhouse Religion).

Goliath would play up his faith and use his knowledge of the Bible to get churches to give him money that he would use for alcohol or to pay off our rent or utilities, bail him out of jail, or donate a car to him. So when Mrs. Rogers came to the door and invited us children to church, I looked at her not as an angel at the time, but as a pawn that Goliath would use. I pitied her for being so blind and naive, but it was me that was blind and naive. This was one of those times in life I sure am glad I was wrong. She was my hope, my sign...my angel.

This gracious blessing from God first started out with us children getting a reprieve for a few hours by going to church on Sunday mornings. Goliath wouldn't go, so it was just us children. The Sunday school teachers would bring us food to eat while we learned about Jesus and God (it was a southern Baptist church, so we didn't talk much about the Holy Spirit). Not only would we get food, but also candies and sodas, and as much as we wanted! I didn't have to reserve some back for my siblings, as I knew their bellies were getting filled just the same as mine, but more importantly, so was our spirit and resolve. After a few months, Mrs. Rogers started a youth choir, which really consisted of us four children and two others from church, which meant choir practice Sunday evenings and at least one day a week after school. More reprieve and time spent with those who fed us, spoiled us, were kind to us... loved us.

The church grounds also held over 20 cabins, a massive mess hall, a pavilion, and much more that they used for Vacation Bible Camps. We had spent previous summers watching from the front yard of our prison, seeing the children laugh and play while having the time of their lives. We would watch them all day like an outsider peering into the window of a perfect family dinner filled with laughter and love. That year, the church paid for each of us to go to Bible Camp during the day. That year at camp was when I became saved and knew I had found my true rescuer! I went back home with ammunition and faith, and while I was still scared at night, I would pray to God, and the room seemed less dark as the power of the monsters and Satan diminished at the mere utterance of God or prayers to God.

Back in the late 80s and early 90s, food stamps came in booklets similar to printed money, but with dull colors. Each booklet was a different denomination, such as $5, $10, $50, etc. They were easily exchangeable for real money or other goods, as well as easy to steal and use. Goliath would often trade them for alcohol, leaving us with little food and without a way to get more until the following month. So, Mrs. Rogers arranged for a person who drove a taxi to pick me up on food stamp day; that day every month, I would pretend to get on the bus and then hide out at the church until the mail arrived. I would take several of the "dollars" out of the back of each booklet so that Goliath wouldn't realize it until he had been drinking and would think it was his doings. Once I had the food stamps, I would get in the taxi with Mrs. Rogers and the church member. They would take me to the grocery store and help me purchase food I could easily smuggle in and prepare for us without the need for the stove: a lot of potted meat or Spam, crackers, bread, corn flakes, powdered milk, jerky, etc. She would store them in the camp's mess hall, which was directly across the road from my house. So that on days when we didn't have any food, I could sneak over and grab enough for us to eat that day. She made sure to include hygienic items that we needed to stay clean.

Most of all, she instilled God's love in me. She taught me the story of Shadrach, Meshach, and Abednego. She also taught me about Jonah and the Whale, Daniel and the Lion's Den, and most importantly, about God's love. How he sent his only Son to rescue me, my Savior Jesus Christ, who came down to earth and died for me. Mrs. Rogers gave me the armor of God, the spiritual armor I needed to survive, be resilient, and yet stay humble with a servant's heart. Here I was, unwanted and unloved by the very people who should have loved me unconditionally. I was beaten and cast away for things I was blameless for, deemed unworthy, yet here was a man named Jesus, the Son of God, who knew exactly how I felt because he was treated the same. He was royalty and because of him, God adopted me. I was royalty. An heir of God, the creator of all, loved me... me! Despite the fact, I would be an orphan in the coming years, I was in fact an heir to a kingdom, the greatest kingdom of all and HIS daughter, who would inherit riches far beyond the imagination. A father who would never hurt, misuse, or mistreat me, who was faithful and never broke his promises. Who claimed me as his child, deemed perfect and blameless by the cleansing of Jesus. He broke the chains of sin and death, and he would be the one to help me become free of my generational chains. When I looked in the mirror, I no longer saw a frail, skinny girl with covered-up bruises and plainness. There was no more fear or shame as a Leftover Sandwich, there was only a warrior like an ancient Viking. A warrior covered in a holy armor full of determination, fierce spirit, and a supernatural joy from the Holy Spirit residing in me. No longer did I dream of a knight in shining armor riding in to save me, Jesus saved me and I had the Holy Spirit within me, Mrs. Rogers and Sampson beside me, and God's armor on me. I was my own hero… and I was ready for battle.

Refined Silver

... to bestow on them a crown of beauty instead of ashes, the oil of joy instead of mourning, and a garment of praise instead of a spirit of despair. They will be called oaks of righteousness, a planting of the LORD for the display of his splendor."

Isaiah 61:3

~ 5 ~

Days are filled with sisterly melodies like "Time Marches On" and "Strawberry Wine," church, working odd jobs like babysitting and house cleaning. One of the neighbors who hired me to clean their house donated a bunch of second-hand toys and books, including a full set of encyclopedias. I now credit a lot of my intelligence to those encyclopedias, but oh how I hated them at the time. When I would get in trouble but not enough for more severe punishments, I would have to read them or the Bible as punishment.

My mouth always got me in trouble (those that know me feign surprise), and it never failed—I would hear the dreaded punishment. Go read Letter C, the first 5 pages, Go read Gi-Gr, read Job 1-8, and so on. Then I would have to recite something I had learned from the pages. Goliath was Mensa intelligent and could read all the pages in an instant and recall any sentence, so he knew if I skimmed the pages or actually read them. Between those horribly wonderful encyclopedias and having to read and memorize passages from the Bible, my non-violent punishments were daunting to a child, but oh how blessed I am for it now! I don't know if Goliath knew how important education in Christ and knowledge were or if it was just a punishment. Regardless, he gave me one of the greatest lessons and gifts in my life: a strong academic foundation of knowledge. I spent so many countless hours in those books that I can still smell the pages and feel the texture of the covers when I close my eyes. Wherever they are now, they have bits of my soul, tears, and heart bound to every page and snarky comments written in the corners. The contents of those donated boxes of books not only gave another form of discipline; they also offered imagination, knowledge, and fun—all at our fingertips.

We would spend cold or rainy days and hours on end in the basement playing with the toys or up in the attic rooms reading and playing make-believe, where we often recreated characters and plots from the stories. I discovered a portal to other worlds in the boxes of books, and I found an escape to worlds all over. Riding a boxcar with Violet, outwitting Fagan with Oliver, building a city with Lisa and Todd, defending rights with Atticus, and helping orphanages with Mother Teresa, as well as countless other adventures. Each book left an imprint on my soul, imprinted with values, lessons, knowledge, justice, humor, and even mischief.

At the bottom of that box, lay my soon-to-be favorite book, a book that I'm convinced God knew I needed. A book that would fill the void of not having a mother. The one thing every little girl needed, and the one thing I knew I would never have again since she died, leaving me to raise myself and three children because our incapacitated father couldn't. A book about a beautiful mother destined to change the world, to fight for people with grace and class, to be elegant and regal while breaking the mold of convention.

The book was none other than a biography of Princess Diana. I would spend every evening pouring over the pages, reading over and over every word about her life as though new words would magically appear between the lines. I was mesmerized by the pictures of her beauty, class, and the amazing mother she was to Prince William and Prince Harry. When I finished, I would start again, over and over, as though there were new nuggets of information I had missed previously. Sometimes just staring for what seemed like hours, transfixed by the photos of her and the young princes playing in the fields or walking along rocks, all of them laughing and experiencing so much love. I would fantasize that she was my mother, that I was somehow lost at birth, that I belonged to her and not the desolate, violent life I was living. I was convinced that any day she would come and save me. We would be reunited, and she would squeeze me in a big hug like she did her children in the book. She would teach me all the things a mother does; she would brush my hair, paint my nails, and sing songs to me in her soft voice. I would get to experience what a hair salon was, have beautiful dresses, and spend late nights giggling after bedtime stories. Most of all, I would have an abundance of safety and love. What could be safer than living in a castle as the granddaughter of a noble Queen? I was convinced I was a modern-day Cinderella, as I would spend my days and evenings fantasizing about it, confident I was about to be transformed into the long-lost princess. I went as far as to place a pebble under my mattress to see if I could feel the difference when I slept so that when Princess Diana came to get me, I could pass the Queen's test. Plot twist...I couldn't, but would visualize it in my head to try to force myself into believing I could.

When Goliath raged, I would just think of Princess Di holding me and wiping the blood away, bandaging my wounds, and wrapping my arm as she embraced me in one of her hugs with that thousand-watt smile that could melt the icecaps. When the neighborhood kids would call me names for being poor, I would just dream of being royalty, and I felt sorry for them that they were not able to see the royalty I really was. I would spend the summer days lying on the ground watching for planes to fly over, imagining she was coming to rescue me. When I saw one, I would jump up and holler towards the sky, "Here I am, Mom, while flailing my arms. Come and get me and let's go to Disneyland."

Refined Silver

It sounds crazy, I know, but Princess Diana, whom I never met... saved my heart. She kept me inspired and putting one foot in front of the other, day after day. When I make it to heaven, I hope to find her and thank her for having such a profound impact on my life. She taught me how to care for others and to follow your heart, even if it wasn't popular. That one person could change the world, she changed the world for so many people. She changed mine. She gave me my first experience of having a dream, a forward vision of a better life, a female role model to mimic and aspire to. She gave me one of the greatest gifts: she gave me hope. Since I was convinced I was royalty because well, she was my mother, I never wanted to dishonor the crown, so I made sure to conduct myself accordingly. From drinking with my pinky up to always being honest, the royalty illusion kept me on the straight and narrow and biding my time. The fantasy kept me grounded while also keeping my head in the sky.

Those boxes of donated toys and books taught me that books are powerful! In them, one can find the greatest adventures, education, imagination, hope, joy, and even fall in love with a stranger. Then one day, life forever changed and my pumpkin was transforming into my carriage. I got off the school bus, as I notice there is a car in the driveway with Kentucky plates on it, but I don't really think much about it. I walk in to find my "dead" mother, like Lazarus, alive and well, resurrected from the dead.

2.0, with my grandparents sitting beside her. It didn't register at first who she was; she looked like me, though I couldn't place where I knew her, but I remembered my Nanny Emily and certainly couldn't forget Joe, so I just stood there confused and frozen in place. They are talking, but I don't hear any words, as though I am in a bubble, and I see them moving their mouths but I can't hear them. At some point, someone asks me if I know who that is, and I reply that I think I know Nanny Emily and Joe. She looks like the woman in my memories of my grandmother, just a little older, but did I make all of this up? It's been over 6 years since I saw her, but that is the only one I think I know. Nanny Emily tells me Spice is my mother, and they have came to see us. Excuse me??? They repeat it, and it still doesn't register. Goliath tells me to go give my mother a hug, and that's when it finally hits me: She is alive!

But time had not been kind; neither had the years of drugs and abuse, so here sat a person resembling the young, vibrant woman I once knew. Now beaten by drugs, men, and life, she was scarred, missing teeth, with a sunken face. The ones not missing were rotting from the drugs and cigarettes, and she just looked like a physical form of stress. Here sat a shell of the vibrant person I remembered. Where has she been? Why did she abandon us? How can she be here... after all this time?

Refined Silver

    They leave that evening with the promise of seeing us again soon, but Goliath tells us afterwards that will never happen. He will not let it. The fear and rage in his eyes shown desperation, like a cornered rabid animal. I knew what that meant—we were moving. Goodbye church and Mrs. Rogers. Good bye food and help... goodbye being loved. 7The following day, a social worker is at the house when I get off the school bus, and she is asking each of us children questions, looking through the cabinets, bedrooms, etc. That was something I was used to; after dozens of previous experiences with family services, I knew what words to avoid and what facade to follow. We had been shown time and time again that telling the truth about what happened in that house would not do anything but anger Goliath even more. Even though they said it was a secret and they wouldn't tell, that they would keep us safe, they always told. Yet, they were never there to keep us safe from his wrath once he found out. But this time was different. A few days later, the same social worker shows up at school and says we have been placed in foster care and it's time to go meet our foster parents. But, for the first time in my life, we weren't going to have each other. No one could take four children, so that meant divide and conquer was the strategy put in place. I was alone in one home, my two sisters were together in another, and my baby brother was in a different one.

Refined Silver

My world shattered; they needed me... I needed them. We followed the script, we were good kids, we made good grades, and we never got in trouble outside of Goliath's unprovoked punishments. Why are we being punished? Ripping us apart was the most agonizing pain I could possibly imagine at that point, yet they didn't seem to care. I was the long-lost princess, Princess Diana was supposed to come get me, and my siblings and I were supposed to have a better life. This is all wrong! The social worker told me to stop crying and smile because I wouldn't want my foster parents to think I wasn't grateful to be there, and that I had to make a great first impression.

So there I stood with a trash bag in my hand, waiting to meet my foster parents, crushed beyond words, fighting back the tears as my heart was in a million pieces. The first thing I notice is a school bus in the yard and two beaming people with thousand-watt smiles. Their eyes sparkled with kindness, and the woman smelled sweet as she embraced me with the warmest of hugs. The man stands there with his hands in his pockets, a pen and a little notepad in his shirt pocket, smiling as he speaks with this softness that radiates to your heart. The social worker introduces me to my foster parents, the Millers.

Often times, when I would meet my new foster parents, the smiles were fake, with every word or action a superficial falsity of niceness and caring. Like a car salesman trying to convince you that you didn't get a lemon. But the Millers were different. They weren't lemons. They were more like the sweetest, coldest glass of lemonade while swinging on the porch on a hot summer day. They were old souls that you have known forever, full of genuine love, kindness, and compassion. You just knew you were home, like walking into Grandma's house as she is taking her fresh, warm chocolate chip cookies out of the oven.

We walk in through the garage, and there is a salon in the back of the garage. Holy smokes! For a girl who had never even had a haircut or even looked in the window of a hair shop, this was surreal and the mark of royalty in my mind. As we walk in and do a tour of my new home, there are two living rooms and two eating areas, curtains on the windows, and some kind of royal sorcery. Within 24 hours, I went from living in a house with trash bags covering the windows to being middle class. They take me to my bedroom, and it's all mine: a full-size cathedral bed with fluffy Ross brand teddy bears along the ruffled pillows, a matching dresser and chest with a TV, and a full-size bathroom attached to it.

My meagerly filled trash bag looks so out of place on the bed, with its sparse contents of panties and socks with holes in them, too-small outfits, or oversized shirts with stains. Fitting, as it is indicative of how I feel standing in this gorgeous house with these loving people. Outwardly, out of place and discarded, but internally, mismatched with scars and holes throughout my heart and soul. The internal struggle of being placed in a foster home is one that words can't capture. I never want to leave this warm and safe place, but I'm so devastated to not have my siblings. Are they hungry, sad, or scared? Who is going to sing them back to sleep when they have a nightmare? I can't keep them safe; I can't protect them. I don't even know where they are. I feel so conflicted and torn into a million pieces as I'm silently crying out to God that I need him to come down and glue the pieces back together. One the one hand, I'm safe and the Millers are so nice. On the other hand, this is a new place with new rules. I woke up in my own Ned this morning and now here I am sleeping in a stranger's bed. I miss my siblings and in spite of the abuse, I even miss Goliath. I grieve my life, gone is summer camp, singing in the church choir. Will someone tell them we are gone? Will they miss us like I miss them? Is Goliath heart broken or is he relieved? Is this all happening because Spice showed up? Lord, please don't send me back to be around Joe.

Mrs. Miller comes in to brush my hair and tuck me into bed for the night. I've never experienced bedtime rituals before, outside of tucking my younger siblings into bed. She asks me if I want her to leave the bathroom light on, and I quietly tell her no, even though every part of me wants to yell yes. Their bedroom is across the hall, and she tells me to come and get her if I need anything or if I get scared, and then it's just myself and my thoughts all alone in my room.

I've never been alone before. I've always had someone to talk to, play with, and at least share a room with. The silence is deafening, my heart aches, and I feel so empty. There is a window to the left of my bed. I can see the night sky from my pillow. The moon is full and cascading down onto my bed. The man in the moon is my only friend tonight. Maybe my siblings are looking at the moon at this same time. Perhaps if all of us look at it at the exact time, I can send my thoughts to them. I spend the next couple of hours silently talking to the moon like I'm talking to my siblings. I tell them I love them and not to be sad or scared. I tell them not to cry and remind them how brave they are. I talk about how this is an adventure like the ones I read to them in our books. As I'm consoling them, I'm in urn consoling myself without even realizing it. I make a silent pact to look up at the moon every night when I go to sleep, so they know I'm thinking of them. Having spoken to my siblings through the moon, I feel a little less lonely and scared. I sneak out of bed and turn on the bathroom light before climbing back into bed to drift off to sleep, all alone in my great big bed. Goodnight Moon. The next morning I wake to the smell of fried bologna, scrambled eggs, and freshly sliced tomatoes. I open my eyes, thinking I'm still at Goliath's, until my eyes come into focus to see beautiful bedroom furniture and the sun cascading onto my bed. I'm

Refined Silver

at the Millers, and that delicious smell of food isn't a dream. In an instant, I go from being excited about having a warm breakfast, to sadness and dread. Am I allowed to get out of bed or do I wait until someone comes in here to get me? If I wait, I may miss breakfast, or maybe they will think I'm lazy. However, if I get up and go into the kitchen when I'm not supposed to, I may get in trouble. What does trouble look like here? Will they hit me or withhold food as punishment like Goliath? Oh God, what if I am molested?! I don't even know if I can go to the bathroom; they might hear the toilet flush causing them to know I'm awake. I don't want to make them angry. My social worker told me not to upset them. She must know something I don't. What if they are horrible and put out cigarettes on my body like Goliath or Renegade? I am uncertain what to do. My stomach rumbles loudly; the smell of the food makes my hunger even worse until I can't stand it any longer. I finally convince myself to risk getting in trouble in search of breakfast. I sheepishly walk into the kitchen to see Mrs. Miller standing over the stove flipping the bologna. She walks over to me and gives me a tight hug, wishes me good morning, and flashes her beautiful smile. Mr. Miller asks me how I slept as he sits at the breakfast table with his cup of coffee and a newspaper. I nervously sit down at the breakfast table, afraid to speak or even move, when he slides the comics page over to me and smiles with his eyes. Within minutes, breakfast is on the table, grace has been said and food is being scooped onto my plate. They tell me

I can get as much as I want, that there is plenty. This is going to be OK. After breakfast, I finally get up enough nerve to ask if I can call my siblings. Much to my surprise, she said yes and calls my social worker to get their number. Hearing my siblings' voice instantly brings tears to my eyes. They sound great, and they are loving their new foster homes. Hearing this comes with mixed emotions. On the one hand, it helps me to know they aren't sad or lonely. On the other hand, though, it's a gut punch because we are separated, and instead of being sad, they appear to be happy. Are they not as devastated as I am? How am I both happy and sad? Maybe they are too?

It was a whirlwind week. One moment I was with Goliath and my siblings, living in that abusive world, and then suddenly I was placed in the polar opposite. The two worlds are so opposite of each other that they are almost enemies. On one side, you have all you've ever known, including parents battling addiction, violence, poverty, and frequent visits from the Department of Family Services and the police. On the other side, you have middle-class America with meat at every meal, nice clothes, dentist appointments, caring parents, sleep without fear of abuse, and parents living a Christian life. Is this going to be forever or will I be sent back to Goliath's? My world was like a snow globe that had been shaken. What will it look like when everything settles?

Refined Silver

A father to the fatherless, a defender of widows,
is God in his holy dwelling. God sets the lonely in families.....

Psalm 68:5-6A

~ 6 ~

What a blessing the Millers were, not only as a physical safe haven but a blessing to my heart and instrumental in my walk with Christ. It wasn't an overnight revelation but their patience and understanding through the process of foster care allowed me to discover the love and grace of God on my own. I missed my siblings greatly and spent many nights in the early weeks crying myself to sleep because we were separated. But in the daylight, the freedom of not having to be responsible for everyone was a weight lifted. The more I would enjoy myself or feel ok, the more I would wrangle with guilt throughout the day and practically suffocate on it every night.

Nights are always the worst because it's just you, the silence and your mind. During the day, you can distract yourself with business while you push your thoughts and feelings to the back burner. The up and down of emotions was nauseating. I would feel lighter because I was able to be a kid, but in the next moment I would feel the weight of the heaviness with worry over my siblings. The heaviest weight was the guilt for being happy at times, the perceived betrayal of my siblings burdened my heart and soul plagued my thoughts.

Refined Silver

I could go to sleep without fear of violence, molestation or something happening to my siblings or me. Yet, the loneliness of being ripped apart, unknowing about their foster home, if they were happy or feeling as lonely as I did hit the hardest at night. I would lie in bed looking out at the moon, earnestly hoping that they also were looking at the moon at the same time as if we could be connected in that moment and they could feel my love from them even separated.

The sheer mental game your heart and mind plays on you when in foster care is almost indescribable. You are introduced to the reality of how broken your previous home was, as though your eyes are opened for the first time. Things you never even viewed in a negative light are glaring obvious. Such as the first time in my life, I was able to take a bath with fresh bathwater still warm out of the faucet that was crystal clear. It may not seem like much but it was a rag to riches tale to me. Here I was in my double digits of age and had never experienced warm clean bath water just for me.

Every since I could remember, my siblings and I shared the same bathwater, my baby brother and youngest sister would go first in water that was lukewarm at best. It barely rose to the middle of the tub even with two children splashing in it. When they were finished, it would be my middle sister and my turn in the now used, cloudy mixture of dirt, grime and urine from my baby brother, no longer lukewarm but now frigid cold bathwater. We would have to sit crisscross applesauce for our long lanky legs to have room for the both of us and if we turned the faucet on, even for a second we were spanked. I still remember the sting and sound of being spanked on a cold wet naked butt and promptly plopped back down into the cool bathwater, at which point I was thankful it was cold as it soothed my burning backside. Trust me, being spanked on your wet hinny bare handed stings as though you sat on a fire log. It not only stings but the pain gradually intensifies for a bit as well. Then instantly pushed back down into the tub of cold water, my body would cause my lungs to suck in the air in choppy sessions as my body and brain were trying to adjust to my senses.

The first few nights Mrs. Miller ran my bath, I was too afraid to tell her it was too hot or too cold when she asked until I learned it was ok and she was genuinely asking how I preferred it. The first time I ever stretched out my legs in the bathtub, was like moving from a Pre-K mat to a California king bed. Every time I would stretch out my legs, "Moving On Up to the East Side" would play in my head. I had moved up in the world.

BTW, if you just sang that sentence in your head, this is your reminder that it's time for night cream... you're welcome.

Refined Silver

The Miller's grandchildren were my age and came over often since they lived behind us a little distance up the gravel road. The grandchildren helped with the loneliness and guilt of my siblings not living with me. I wasn't an only child when they were around; when it was just me, it was a stark reminder my siblings weren't with me. Lily, James, and I spent long summer evenings racing each other up and down the gravel road, gorging on subs as long as the table, and turning everything into a game, a lesson, or mischief.

Lily and I would play make-believe while James and I would make everything a competition. We would compete to see who could swing the highest or hang from the bars the longest; you name it, we made a competition out of it. With them, I was free to feel my emotions. When I was sad, Lily would smile the biggest smile that would melt the sadness like an ice cream cone on a hot summer day. If anyone could compete with Princess Diana's smile....it was Lily. While James pushed me to explore adventures and made everything a competition, even standing side by side to which of us had the longest legs. I'm not sure which of us hated to lose the most, but he always beat me at racing and I always beat him with the longer legs. He was smart, and taught me it was ok to be smart, even if others thought it was nerdy. They helped me form my personality by loving and accepting me, warts and all.

Refined Silver

Tim (Lily and James' father) and Shane were like fun uncles instead of just brothers because of the age gap. They always let us get away with an extra piece of candy or drink or fast food (which was foreign to me beforehand). Tim was secretly my favorite. I always felt safe and secure with him around and loved to hear his laugh. I would think of ways to make him laugh just so I could hear it and laugh along with him. He was such a loving and playful dad to Lily and James that I would just watch them in admiration and jealously as I wished I had that relationship.

Mr. Miller, Tim, and Shane were the complete opposite of any male I had known to that point. They were patient, kind, strong, and protective, but in the most calming, reassuring way. Every man I had known before was angry, arrogant, stern, and manipulative. It was as though I went from one life to an alternative universe. In this one, I was loved and cherished, safe and secure. I was happy....I was loved.

Mrs. Miller was in nursing school and would have her books strewn across the dining room table, highlighting notes and studying, while Mr. Miller and I would sit at the round breakfast table. He hopelessly and patiently tried to make math understandable to me. Even with his best effort, it made zero sense to me, and all I wanted to do was run and play in the yard or play Dr. with Mrs. Miller's pressure cuff and stethoscope. Still to this day, numbers make little sense to me, yet literature is magical like music to my soul. (Sorry Dad, you tried, it's me—not you.)

The math lessons may not have stuck, but the lessons he taught me about what a Godly man consists of did. Oh how I wish I could rewind at times and just go back to sitting at the breakfast table with Mr. Miller and his little shirt pocket with a mini pad and pen, futilely explaining math to me. I can close my eyes even now and be teleported back to that time. I still can feel the coolness of the garage and the frigid cold shampoo bowl as I sat ecstatic because Mrs. Miller was perming my hair. In the mornings, she would brush my hair and braid it or put it in a half bun. She would make me breakfast or pour me a bowl of cereal every morning. I felt like a princess, one no longer lost; I had found home. I had finally found my mother, a woman who was classy, loving, and had the warmest of hugs. We spent hours riding in the car jamming out to the Statler Brothers about having a little talk with Jesus, with Mrs. Miller tapping her fingers in rhythm on the steering wheel and singing along with her beautiful voice. They both drove my school bus, though usually it was Mr. Miller. On days when it was warm, I would sit on the front porch swing waiting for him to pick me up, as I was never ready when he was making his first round. So he would head up the hill and pick me up on the way down.

Refined Silver

Watching the sunrise over the mountains while swinging on the porch swing, just God and I, were some of the most peaceful memories I have ever had. Watching the sun rise between the mountain peaks, the sky changing colors every second was my time worshipping God and his creation. A moving art piece that Picasso or Van Gogh could paint would pale in comparison to the breathtaking views God created daily. No longer did I search for planes with Princess Diana; instead I would just swing back and forth, thanking God for his glorious ways.

Mornings in the winter were so cold, so Mr. Miller would go start the bus early and pick me up on the way back down the hill so I could stand in the warmth of the house while I eagerly watched out the front door for my ride. I would try to soak up as much heat as possible and race to the bus before the heat dissipated from my body and the cold would smack me. Like a human rechargeable battery. Spoiler alert—it never worked. But I did always get to pick whichever seat I wanted since I was the first on, or I would tell Mr. Miller which one I wanted and he would save it for me. In the evenings, I was always the last one off, just Mr. Miller and I bouncing around as the bus barreled down the mountain and around the curves. That is serious power for a school kid, and no one bullied me because my foster dad was the one in charge. But that had a downside too: if I got in trouble, he would call my name, and I would have to come sit in the seat behind him so he could keep an eye on me. It was embarrassing, yet when I would look up in that long mirror, I would see those warm eyes behind his aviator glasses wrinkle up, and he would flash a smile that softened the rebuke. He taught me there were consequences to my actions but still did it in a loving way, far different from my prior experiences with other foster homes and my home life. In the evenings, when it was just us and the empty bus, we would pretend it was a roller coaster. I would close my eyes and put my hands up in the air to simulate a roller coaster as we made our way down the winding mountains of Virginia. No matter how bad a day I had at school, it would melt away the moment the bus transformed into a carnival ride, with Mr. Miller and I laughing through it all.

The Millers would study the Bible with me and taught me more in depth about God's mercy, Jesus' saving grace, and the Holy Spirit's guidance. They took me to every church event with them, but more importantly, they emulated the life of a follower of Christ. They were teaching me not just with the Word of God but also through their actions and humbling nature. On Oct. 6th of that year, I was baptized and proudly declared to the world that I was a follower of Christ forever. I had envisioned this transformation to be like an ugly duckling turning into a swan when you came out of the water. Plot twist... the water is just water. Outwardly, I was the same just wet. Inwardly, it was a different story. My heart swelled with pride, not the arrogant kind of pride; the joyful kind. Like when a parent is filled with pride when their child walks for the first time. I felt like climbing to the highest mountaintop and announcing to the world, that Jesus Christ is King and I am his! My soul jumped for joy as I was finally where I belonged both physically and spiritually.

Refined Silver

Count it all joy, my brothers, when you meet trials of various kinds, for you know that the testing of your faith produces steadfastness. And let steadfastness have its full effect, that you may be perfect and complete, lacking in nothing.

James 1:2-4 ESV

Refined Silver

~ 7 ~

Life was great! I had visitations with my siblings often, where we would spend hours playing along with non-stop bragging to each other about all the things we had done with our foster families. Though we were separated, everyone was content in our new normal, happy lives. My sisters were in one foster home, The Smiths, while my baby brother and I were separately in others. The Smiths were overjoyed to have my sisters in their home and treated them like royalty. They bought my sisters' expensive gowns and put them in pageants, with shiny shoes, puffy hair, makeup, and all the works. My sisters acted like royalty as well (insert eye roll). If the Grinch's heart grew three times its size with acceptance and love, my sisters' heads grew the same way. They spent their weekends riding on four-wheelers, horses, and going on picnics with my brother's foster family, The Whitemores, when they weren't parading across the pageant stage.

The Whitemores were related to the Smiths, so they all spent quite a bit of time together throughout the week. My brother never truly felt alone which was important to me since we was in a home by himself. While I lived on the other side of the county, I was blissful and ecstatic where I was. Home is where the heart is, and the Millers were home. We were the all-American family. I had received the Presidential Achievement Award from President Clinton and I sang in the all-state choir. The Millers supported me and were proud of me, no matter what I achieved. All four of us were living the life we had always wanted. We are all well adjusted and thriving. Talks of adoption are now a common occurrence, and the state tells everyone it's for sure going to happen. The Smiths are the first to spearhead the adoption conversation. With their abundance of wealth and influence, it only made sense for them to lead. Conversations of money and high "adoption" fees bring out our biological parents as they try to extort large sums of money in exchange for willingly signing over parental rights. The amount grows larger and larger until there is a stalemate and talks fall through. So we adjust to being foster kids without an option for adoption. It's not that big of a deal to us because we are just going to stay where we already are until we become adults anyway. Until I come home from school one day and I can tell Mrs. Miller has been crying, the warmth in Mr. Miller's eyes has been replaced with sadness. Something is wrong....terribly wrong.

Mrs. Miller explains to me that I have been placed in another foster home and I have to finish packing my belongings because it's happening tonight. I didn't understand, did I do something wrong? I promise I will work harder at math and not be so difficult to teach. I'll get up on time and ride the bus without complaint, even when it's super cold. I'll do anything. Please don't make me go! I pleaded, cried, and bartered, but to no avail. The decision was not ours, and it was final. Someone who never spoke to me, who didn't even know my name passed down the ruling, and it was final. How can he or she decide what's best for me when they don't even know who I am? What did I ever do to warrant this? The Millers were going to be my forever parents; my siblings were royalty. Didn't someone tell the powers that be? All these thoughts and more race through my head like they are mimicking the speed of light. I'm handed a beautiful teddy bear that's sat on my bed since I arrived, given a tear-soaked, boa-constricting tight hug, and then I'm gone.

That night, I am taken to the Holts, my new foster home. They were older, stoic, dry, and strict. There's no welcome, no getting accustomed to each other. Instead, I am greeted with a list of rules and shown to my room in the basement. In the tiny room stood a small bed with one dresser that held a single lamp. No windows, no light, just four suffocating walls. The room was as cold as my new foster parents. Dinner time had already passed, so there was nothing to eat until the next morning. From the moment I arrive, I am banished to my cold and lonely room. I cried myself to sleep. I begged God to make it right. Please Lord, make this all a bad dream and wake me up!

Refined Silver

The heartache and tears originate in a place far deeper than I have ever experienced. The pain is so deep that it physically hurt to breathe in.

When I was first placed with the Millers, it felt as though I was in a snow globe that had been shaken. This was different; the snow globe has been shattered, and the glass shards that figuratively lay on the ground couldn't cut deeper than the pain I feel. I ask to call the Millers; I just need to hear their voice, but I am told they don't want to talk to me. Throughout the week, I'm not allowed to leave my bed when not at school, except to do chores, take a quick shower, use the bathroom, or eat dinner. On the weekends, I'm allowed to play outside in the backyard, but none of the foster parents' biological children want to talk or play with me. So I just sit outside on the grass, trying to make my soul feel warm again, as though the sun can magically give me that.

It's one thing to be removed from everything you have known and shoved into a place with strangers. It's another thing to be dropped into a place where you aren't even wanted. You are a foreigner who speaks a different language. You don't know the rules of the place you are in, but you're expected to follow them without fail the instant you arrive. You can't get ahead because you don't even know the culture or background. On top of that, there's not even an indifference towards you, instead its disgust and pity at your plight. In a time when you need to be comforted and supported, you feel isolated, scared, and alone.

Picture yourself walking through a middle-class community in a foreign country during a torrential downpour. You see a picturesque window with a joyous family having dinner, warm and secure. You stand in front of the window, watching everything transpire, close enough to smell the food and hear the laughter and whispered conversations. You see everything you wish you had but don't; they are aware you are there, but you are not invited in. Instead, they bring you a slice of bread and then leave you in the rain, and then they pat themselves on the back for the charity provided. Being in an uncaring foster home is a lot like that.

You are on the outside looking in, and it's made crystal clear that you are an inconvenience with a paycheck. No one speaks to me except to taunt me and make sure that I know I'm unwanted, unloved, and unworthy. I feel like I have been handed down a sentence of hard time in maximum security prison, but for the life of me, I don't know what crime I have committed. My only crime was being born to my biological parents. Not only am I in prison, I'm in solitary confinement. There is no TV, no friend, nothing but my Teddy Bear and me. He was now my sole companion, a reminder of my happy life that no longer existed, the life I had prior to my prison sentence.

Weeks go by, and my days and nights are always the same. I go to school; I come home and sitting on my bed until chore time. Then back to sit on my bed until I am called for dinner; afterwards, I clean the kitchen, take a 5-minute shower, and am sent back to my room. The pain hits like a tidal wave every night. I yearn to be comforted, to see or talk to the Millers just for a minute. There is no one but my Teddy, God, and myself. So with my teddy bear on my chest, I curl up in a ball around him, I cry, and I rock myself for hours on end until I cry myself to sleep, wake up the next morning, and do it all over again.

After a month or so, my baby brother has been moved into the home with me. But he is put in a different part of the house where girls are not allowed to be. We rarely saw each other except for waiting for the bus, dinner, and the occasional playtime outdoors. But at least he was nearby. He gave me strength by being there because I knew I had to take care of him.

The Holts had a son, T.J., who was just a year younger than me, but he was the biggest jerk I had ever met. When my brother was placed in the home, T.J. had to share a room with him, and T.J. hated that. Being a foster kid was like being a Muggle in Hogwarts, as though poverty and abuse victimhood were contagious and they might catch it from us. So he began to pick on my brother and bully him any chance he got. Every time I would see my brother, he was always upset and crying because of the relentless tormenting. When he told the Holts about the bullying from T.J., nothing was done to stop it, which only encouraged T.J. to step up the tormenting. We were outside one day and I saw T.J. push my brother over and hold him down while making him slap himself. Mockingly saying, "Stop hitting yourself," while my brother pleaded for him to stop. This, of course, resulted in a bloody nose. Not my brother's....T.J.'s. I ran over to him as I screamed for T.J. to get off of my brother. He stood up and asked me what I was going to do about it, saying he wasn't too afraid to hit a girl. He apparently wasn't too afraid to be hit by a girl either because, before I knew it, I had made direct contact that echoed a pop and crunch sound that seemed to roll across the mountainous backdrop. My fist landed right across the bridge of his nose and broke it, which landed me in the crosshairs of the Holts and our social worker. It further ostracized my brother and I in the home, but that was the last time he ever laid a hand on my brother, and it was clear he was indeed...now afraid of a girl.

I continued asking to call the Millers or write to them; I was always told they didn't want to hear from me. Usually no explanation was given; it was just a matter of fact that they didn't want to hear from me. It never made sense because I was supposed to live with them forever. They told me they loved me and always doted on me; they wouldn't just stop loving me. This was a twilight zone, and I was internally screaming that I'm innocent and that I didn't do anything to stop their love for me.

After T.J.'s broken nose, the Holts sat at the dinner table that night and told me I wasn't wanted by the Millers, and they had me removed because I was a problem child and no one wanted me. I look over at TJ, holding a frozen bag of peas on his face, still in his blood-soaked shirt, now with a smug look on his face as they tell me they took my brother and I out of pity because no one else would take us. I found out later that simply wasn't true, but at the time it was a dagger to my heart. It broke me like a wild stallion is broken when saddled... it broke my spirit. I sat in my room mulling over every second I spent with the Millers, dissecting every word I said or everything I did, trying to find out what I did wrong. If I could figure out what I did wrong and why I was unlovable, then I could fix it, and the Millers would love me again. I could be granted clemency and released from this prison.

The Holts and their son made it their mission to remind my brother and I daily that we were charity and came from bad stock, which meant we were bad stock. The emotional damage inflicted was worse than any physical abuse I had ever endured. My soul lay bare, and they just kept hammering at it. To this day, I can't find the words to adequately describe the depth of the despair and heartache I felt. I couldn't take it anymore; my spirit felt like it had been filleted open and severed from all that was good. It hurt to breathe. It hurt to even exist. It just excruciatingly hurt.

I packed my bags one night and called our social worker, bawling, with threats of running away with my brother and them never ever finding us again if we had to stay in that home any longer. I had read The Boxcar Children, and if Violet could do it, so could I. I could raise my siblings on a train and we would be just fine. I didn't know why I was unlovable or unworthy, but I did know I couldn't take this place anymore. The next day, my brother and I were paroled from that prison....but we were released to Goliath.

Refined Silver

But the Lord said to Samuel, "Do not look on his appearance or on the height of his stature, because I have rejected him. For the Lord sees not as man sees: man looks on the outward appearance, but the Lord looks on the heart."

1 Samuel 16:7

~ 8 ~

Within a week of being sent back to Goliath, he moves us to Winston-Salem across state lines to try and escape the court hearings, warrants for his arrest, and social services. He has met someone new, and we move into her place, a HUD-style apartment building square in the middle of the projects. When I say "middle of the hood," I literally mean how Hollywood movies portray the hood. Clothing lines between rows of apartments; drugs, trash, and broken-down vehicles all litter the sidewalks. Gun shots echoing in the background, aggressive hip hop, violent rap music and gang signs everywhere you go. It was unsafe for us to go outside and play for fear of witnessing violence or being the victim of it. Goliath was robbed and beaten more than once, just getting out of his car to walk into the apartment. When we would board the bus in the morning, grandmothers in their house slippers and robes watched over us at the bus stop to ensure we weren't harmed while we waited. In the evenings, drug dealers and gangs were out and active, while neighborhood grandmothers and grandfathers walked us to our homes.

You didn't make eye contact. You exited quickly and ran into your apartment. You don't wander from the group or go to them when they call you to come over, or you stand the risk of them trying to recruit you or worse. "Recruiting" was a polite term I never understood back then because it made it seem like you had a choice, but most often it was more of a "Volun-told" situation, where you were TOLD you were volunteering.

Since my baby brother and I shared a room, we spent a lot of time together. When you can't go outside, you can't be by the window, and you are too poor to afford anything, time together is all there is. Time together was just what we needed, though — we spent months laughing, telling stories, playing rummy, and just enjoying being together again. I would lie in bed at night watching over us for fear of being shot in our sleep or someone breaking in. It's amazing how quickly your body returns to survival mode, just as it did all the years before, as though I never left.

Often times, Goliath and his girlfriend would be gone on drinking binges, so responsibility fell back to me again to wash our clothes, cook dinner, do homework, keep us safe, etc. An upside of living in the inner city is the programs implemented to help give inner city kids a fighting chance, so we took advantage of after-school programs such as karate classes three times a week and art or pottery classes on alternate days. Because every 11-year-old needs to be able to do Bruce Lee's roundhouse kick on Timmy the Gangbanger with his 9 mm and then go make a Picasso art piece.

Refined Silver

Our electricity was disconnected often, and Goliath would turn it back on secretly by utilizing his electrician skills. So he put black trash bags over the windows to keep people from seeing that our electricity was on when it should have been disconnected. We weren't allowed to remove them or peek through the windows. I spent that year thinking the sun vanished because it was dark 24/7. Most kids play games like "The floor is lava." We played a game called "Is it daytime or nighttime?" We didn't know if it was raining or snowing....we didn't even know what season we were in half the time unless you opened the front door.

All the belongings we had amassed while in foster care were pawned or sold, and we were quickly thrown back into poverty: meager rations of food, many bedtimes with belly aches when the meager rations ran out. Most of the time, we survived off of government cheese, peanut butter, and powdered milk. Ninety-nine percent of our food didn't have to be chewed; you just spooned it in and swallowed it. I started to think our teeth were decorations rather than tools.

Since I was thrown back into being my brother's protector and problem solver, there was no point in thinking about the previous years, or how much I wanted to be in a beautiful warm bed surrounded by people who loved me. Instead, my mind couldn't think about anything other than the next four moves to survive. Gone were the days of never being hungry or fearful; instead, the reality was old and bleak. Fantasizing or living in the past was a luxury I didn't have because one slip-up could literally be life or death. While life was hard, there were opportunities presented that would never have been possible without being in the trenches.

Because we lived in the poorest part of the inner city and the 7th most violent city in the US, there were many programs for youth to get an education and stay off the streets. I learned self-defense and karate and progressed through several belt colors. My skin is so pale, it glows in the dark, and where we lived at the time, that was a blinking light like Rudolph's nose, that signaled to my peers that I didn't belong. Karate ended up being what I needed most of all. Not for violence, but to learn self-control, how to deflect and create distance, and how to minimize the damage. I was one of the only two white girls in my entire grade/school, and I was the new girl at that. At first, no one talked to me, and then the "wrong" person talked to me. A bi-racial boy befriended me, and that set the wheels into motion. It was common knowledge that I was to stay in my lane and stick to "where I belonged." But it wasn't common knowledge to me or common to how I was raised, so I had no idea. I had never witnessed racism or had someone hate me or others for the color of my/their skin. I had been bullied for being poor, who my parents were, or being plain Jane. But I never had anyone pick on me because I dressed "like a white girl" or "spoke like a white girl" until I moved there. Apparently, being friends with a popular black guy was a violation that I didn't even know existed. I thought segregation ended decades ago. I thought we were free to befriend, love, or marry anyone we chose because we are all God's creation, his children through Christ, we are all worthy and equal. The pain and hate from the injustice of slavery, segregation, and being treated less than had been passed down through generations and I was the enemy because I was white.

At first, it was just knocking my books out of my hands, shoving me up against the locker with racial slurs like "Cracker," "Wigger," etc. Then it progressed to people running up behind me and jerking me to the ground from behind, yanking me by my hair; running up and hitting me in the face with a school book, then running off; I was spit on and called names. I was threatened that I would be jumped by groups of people when I boarded the bus; anything that could make them look cool or intimidate me and let me know I wasn't welcome, they did it.

My teachers acted afraid, my father was rarely home, and I dared not fight back because I was severely outnumbered. It became so bad, the teachers made me play at recess in a fenced in area separate from the other kids to avoid being jumped. I had to sit with the teachers at lunch in order to ensure I would hurt. I was afraid at school; I was afraid at home, which left me in a perpetual state of fear 24/7.

Sprinkled through it all, God still gave me joyful moments to preserve. My choir and I got to sing for President Clinton. We were able to learn art techniques through after-school classes, we were taught self-discipline through karate and more. But the greatest opportunity was bonding with my baby brother. During that period, we became the best of friends. He was like my own child. Hours upon hours of his comedic relief; evenings and nights of helping him with his school work, bath time, and bedtime stories. It was him and me against the world; we had escaped our solitary confinement foster home, and while this was horrible, at least I knew he was OK because I ensured it. I matured incredibly fast that year because he needed a mother figure—someone worthy of being a role model for him, someone to be a responsible adult to lead and guide him.

One day, a social worker came to school and called me to the office. She said the judge had decided I was moving back to the Bluegrass State as he had awarded Spice custody. I didn't even know they had went to court. I was blindsided by the need. I thought that meant all four of us were going to finally be reunited. She whisked me away to a parking lot, where I saw my youngest sister and her tear-stained face begging to stay with her foster parents. The rest of us are stunned, confused and heartbroken as we discover, we are still going to be separated. Goliath and Spice had come to an agreement; each of them got a pair of us so they could both get equal welfare and government assistance.

That evening, my baby sister and I were headed to Kentucky, and my middle sister and baby brother were headed to North Carolina. The war between Goliath and Spice had ceased, and we (the children) were the collateral damage; still separated, and now the pairing had shifted. There would be no visitations, no phone calls or letters, no back and forth—just forever separated. In the first few months, Spice made sure our time spent was filled with celebrations, promises, joy, and laughter. Spice was still with Renegade, but it seemed to be different. We had our own rooms; food was plentiful and delicious; we spent nights playing cards or games, listening to 80s rock, and catching up. Most of all, we didn't witness any abuse. The honeymoon period didn't last long, as I quickly learned that I had jumped out of the frying pan... into the fire.

Refined Silver

Little children, let no one deceive you. He who practices righteousness is righteous, just as He is righteous. He who sins is of the devil, for the devil has sinned from the beginning. For this purpose the Son of God was manifested, that He might destroy the works of the devil.

1 John 3:7-8 NKJV

~ 9 ~

Like in all domestic violence situations, there are moments of fun and laughter, but the honeymoon stage doesn't last long. The first couple of months were great for getting reacquainted with Spice and spending time with my baby sister again. We spent days playing in the river, making homemade taffy and making cookies in the kitchen for the constant barrage of company that came over to welcome us home. It wasn't the same or as good as it was with the Millers, but maybe it could be a different kind of good. But night time would hit, and I would lie in bed, listening to Selena, and cry myself to sleep, over missing my other sister and baby brother.

Renegade had two cousins who were college football players and were the most abnormally large men I had ever seen. Anakim was the youngest at 20-years-old and always wanted to hang out with me. I thought it was so cool that this college football player wanted to be my friend. He was the closest thing to a celebrity I had ever known. Originally, he would bring his football over and hang out. He taught me how to play football in the front yard or would launch me high above his head into the river when we went for an

Refined Silver

afternoon swim. He began coming around more and more. At the beginning of every visit, he would always go with my parents to their room for a bit. I didn't know what they were doing back there, but I knew we weren't allowed in the back of the house when they were all in the room having coughing fits. Afterwards, the house would stink like a cross between a stinky wet animal and a year-old ashtray. Once they were finished with their business in the backroom, he would watch The Price is Right with me on the couch, take me to his car and play Tupac, or wrestle with me on the living room floor. Shortly afterwards, Spice and Renegade started converting the garage into a smoking room/game room for them and their guests, so Anakim started staying overnight a couple of times a week so he could spend the summer days building the smoking room. He would suddenly be standing in the hall when I got out of the shower or would walk into my room while I lay on my bed in my shorts and sports bra. He never made me feel uncomfortable or like I should be on guard; just acted like a big brother.

Then one day, he gave Spice and Renegade some money to run into town for what I later found out was a drug run. I had been outside playing basketball and running around the neighborhood. I come inside and sit on the fake leather couch in the smoking room, trying to cool off. I am sitting there under the ceiling fan in my shorts and sports bra when Anakim came in. He sits beside me and makes small talk, then asks me if I want to wrestle. I tell him I am too hot and tired to wrestle right now. Shortly after, he begins flicking my hair and thumping me on the leg in hopes of irritating me and causing me to wrestle with him out of frustration. Suddenly, he pushes me down and lays on top of me and starts kissing me. I try to push him away as I ask him what he is doing and tell him to stop it. He continues to hold me down and removes my shorts and panties. I start fighting him even harder, screaming for him to get off of me as it was becoming hard to breathe and I was panicking as I was now naked from the waist down. The weight of him was crushing me to the point where my screams became painful gasps of breathing in and out. He finally allows me to get up, and when I bend down to get my clothes, he pins me against the couch with him behind me.

He tries to rape me, but logistics don't work because my small 90 lb. frame is like a Chihuahua and he is like a junkyard dog that is made up of a Bull Mastiff and a Rottweiler pedigree. I'm crying out in pain, begging him to stop. Between my screams, my bucking and fighting him, and the fact he can't penetrate, it just angers him even more. He becomes more aggressive and demanding and forcefully shoves my face into the couch cushion, to the point where I can taste the pleather in my mouth. The smell of stale cigarettes and marijuana is stifling. I feel like I'm being suffocated and ripped apart at the same time. He holds my face down with one massive hand on the back of my neck. I'm trying to scream for help, but my words are smothered by the tear stained couch.

He is going to kill me. I can't breathe and I can't fight back. I am completely helpless and growing weaker by the minute. My mind races from trying to figure out a way to fight him off to the thought of Spice finding my mostly naked body, raped, bruised, and deceased by the time they get back. Lord, please don't let him kill me or rape me. Please make it stop. My baby sister comes into the house, and he finally gives up. He whispers in my ear that if I say anything, he will hurt her and me. I hurriedly get dressed and rush her and I outside, far away from him, as I try to catch my breath and steady my shaking body.

When Spice and Renegade get back hours later, they join Anakim out in the smoking room, and the coughing fits continue. While getting high, Spice sees bloody scratches on Anakim's face from when I was fighting him and a busted lip from when I head-butted him. Once they come out, I get called into the kitchen and hollered at for being aggressive and hurting him when we were wrestling. I tell Spice we weren't wrestling and that he sexually assaulted me, and tried to rape me, and I fought him every step of the way which resulted in his injuries. She tells me that he told her we were wrestling and that I got upset because he wouldn't kiss me, so I scratched him and head-butted him. She gives me the riot act about how he is a great guy and I'm just making up lies because Goliath taught me to lie. The berating goes on for 20 minutes; I'm such a liar because my father is one; I'm just like my father's side of the family; etc. They make me bend over the very couch Anakim assaulted me on just hours earlier. I'm made to drop my pants and bend over as they spank me with a belt in front of him. There is no way they can't see the already bruised skin and handprint outlines. There's no way they can't see his smug face take delight that he was believed. It was like I was being punished for not just allowing him to do what he wanted. I can't even feel the belt hit me over and over; I just feel anger, devastation, and betrayal.

This moment solidified the knowledge that I was on my own, that the devil was on the prowl and wanted to devour me. I laid in bed that night under two sweatshirts, jeans, and socks, curled up in the corner so I could see both the door and the window in case someone tried to come in. I tried to cover every inch of skin as though the armor of cloth from head to toes would protect me. The bruises were already spreading over my body; they hurt no matter how I sat or laid, the sheer touch of my clothing hurt. It hurt to move. Walking or going to the bathroom was breathtakingly painful. Like when you are riding your bike and you slip off the seat and hit the bar...that moment when you suck in air to try to fill your lungs to alter the pain... that kind of pain.

Every second, every scent, every word, every breath of the horrific ordeal, played in an endless loop in my head. I questioned what I had done wrong. Was it my fault for walking around in a sports bra? Was it my fault for being friendly? Did I laugh the wrong way or smile too long? These and more were questions the devil was using to deceive me into thinking I was responsible in any way. At the time I didn't know, I felt ashamed, dirty, fearful, hurt and devastated. The outward wounds were superficial compared to my soul's deep wounds. The deepest part of me felt like it died a little, a place I didn't even know existed until I felt the weeping sadness that now ached from there. I cried myself to sleep while tightly huddled in the corner, hopeful that tomorrow would be different, that this was all a bad dream.

The following day, Princess Diana was killed in a car wreck, the symbolism not lost on me that my happily-ever-after had died. I searched through all of my clothes for the nicest article of clothing I had. Six days later, I sat in the floor in my best dress, an Easter dress from the Millers. I sat on the red shag carpet in the living room. The carpet permeated the smell of stale cigarettes and marijuana smoke from every fiber from years of indoor smoking.

I tried my best to sit like a proper princess in my dress, but I was bruised all over, it hurt to sit, it hurt to even exist. The physical pain matched the pain of my broken heart as I sat glued to the floor TV as my imaginary mother's casket was carried in. The sound of the pall bearers' shoes upon the marble floor coming out of the speakers on the TV is like nails sealing up my fate in a coffin box. I sat there for hours sobbing as I watched her funeral play out on national television and listened to Elton John sorrowfully belt out Candle in the Wind. As I watched them bury the People's Princess, I too, buried is a piece of my innocence along with my hopes and dreams of a safe place and loving family.

Refined Silver

"What man among you, if he has a hundred sheep and loses one of them, does not leave the ninety-nine in the pasture and go after the one that is lost, until he finds it? And when he finds it, he joyfully puts it on his shoulders, comes home, and calls together his friends and neighbors to tell them, 'Rejoice with me, for I have found my lost sheep!' In the same way, I tell you that there will be more joy in heaven over one sinner who repents than over ninety-nine righteous ones who do not need to repent.

Luke 15:4-7

Refined Silver

~ 10 ~

Spice had surgery on her shoulder and they allegedly messed up so severely, it required muscle and fat from her thigh to fix. She sued them for medical negligence and won a substantial settlement. At about the same time, Renegade went to work high as a kite and wasn't paying attention, which resulted in being "injured" on the job in a forklift accident. He immediately hired a lawyer and began to fake headaches and spells to support his case of head injury. Yet, at home, he was 100% fine; he would party, he spoke perfectly fine, and never once took an aspirin or Tylenol. He also sued and received a settlement. Between the two of them, they collectively had a high six-figure payout within a year of the two suits.

During this time, we received a call from the state that Goliath was arrested in a police raid full of guns and illegal things in the house and we needed to come and get my other siblings as the state had fully taken away his rights. So now all four of us were back together and money wasn't an issue. What could possibly go wrong? Well, when your parents are drug addicts that make poor decisions...a lot. They blew the money on motorcycles, buying a hillside of worthless land that didn't even have a solid water source, all to grow marijuana and put a trailer on it. As well as buying ridiculously worthless expenditures such as an old raggedy white Dodge truck that barely ran and a bulldozer they didn't even know how to operate. Within a year, we were desolate and back on welfare, and the gasoline issues were ever present and then some.

Blame was cast between the two of them over who was responsible for being out of money. And now we have even more mouths to feed. Gone was the protection of being able to run to Lavender's house to call 911. Instead, we now lived in the middle of nowhere, deep in the holler, surrounded by nothing but trees, poverty, and vulnerability. When either of them raged, there was no place to get help, nowhere to run to. We were fish in a barrel.

The men that came around for or with drugs in exchange for being able to sexually assault me didn't stop. The move actually inhibited their ambitions as they could catch me outside with no witnesses or fear of interruptions, or in the shed, pull me deep into the woods, pin me against one of their vehicles, or even lay me over my sister's bed. There was no safe place except for school, and those 6 hours flew by in an instant. Some days, I would get off the bus and one of them would even be waiting. One of them in particular would always sing the song Brandy(you're a fine girl), what a good wife you would be, as though it was his mating call and I knew what that meant. To this day, the song instantly makes me nauseous. Even though I have healed, forgiven and moved on, there are always certain scents, sounds, and situations that take me back. While I logically know I am safe, my body doesn't, and nausea, fear, and agitation will take over in an instant, and I have to fight it to bring me back to the current time. That song is one of those triggers. When they weren't attempting or succeeding in sexually assaulting me, they would make inappropriate comments on how I looked or what I wore, cat calling or whistling, inappropriate touching, etc.

Then Tibbs came along. He was a Hell's Angels biker and supplied their drugs now that they could afford higher quality and even grow his product for him. His wife quickly became friends with Spice and their son, who was my age, became my friend, the only friend I had outside of school at the time. He was my confidante, my refuge in all of that darkness. By the time we were 14, he was a drug transporter for his father and had the clout to pretty much walk into any room and command their attention, at least in the circles our family ran in. I finally found protection from the wolves when we started dating. Out of the fire but into the frying pan. When you are dating a drug runner, you can imagine where that leads. It wasn't long before I was smoking pot with them on the weekends and would be in the car when he went on drug runs. It was such a weird place to be in because he never let me out of the car on these runs and would leave me in the dark to "protect me," yet I wasn't stupid and I knew exactly what he was doing. He had a driver and a buffer who would run interference if he ran into trouble. Anytime we were together, there was a group of guys who would protect me. I knew it was wrong to run with this crowd. I knew I was not where God wanted me to be in life, that I was seeking refuge in a misguided person as opposed to my perfect Father. But suddenly, all these predators were leaving me alone, and here was a boy, vowing no one would ever treat me badly again, professing his love, treating me more than a sex object or punching bag. He was tender, kind to me, and safe.

All the while, the Holy Spirit is telling me this is wrong, that this isn't love or freedom, that walks under the stars aren't compared to being in the presence of the One who makes the stars. However, my mind tells me this was safety and true love, that I could contain the sin, and can keep it from corrupting me. I can only imagine how God must have felt during this time in my life, offering unconditional true love to me and instead I chose the lie of the enemy. That this drug dealing Hell's Angel's son had better love and protection than my Heavenly Father.

For a year, I lived this double life. During the week, I was a good girl, made good grades, did my chores, etc. But the weekend came and I would be partying, getting drunk by a bonfire or smoking pot and playing pool.

Refined Silver

The partying had gotten so bad that one night, after drinking all night, I walked through a bonfire. I woke up the next morning on the ground covered in my own bloody vomit with charred pants and zero recollection of the night before. Friends had to tell me what happened, and even then it was blank. To this day I still have zero recollection. With the history of Goliath and his father's alcohol addiction, I was quickly about to go down the same rabbit hole they did.

At school the week before Valentine's Day, everything I had ever pent up came to a head. Prom was on the horizon, which meant prom proposals. We didn't have the awesome cheesy ones like they do now. Nope, some guy would ask the girl in person at school or over the phone, they would say yes, and that was it... ahh the romance. One of the star basketball players, Marcus, had asked me to prom even though I wasn't a junior or senior, and I politely declined, in part because he had a girlfriend and I a boyfriend, and partly because he imitated a pine tree that hovered over me at 6'2 and a 100 lbs. soaking wet.

Our morning routine was that the bus dropped you off at school anywhere from 20 minutes to an hour before the first bell. You had three options: grab breakfast, hang out in the gravel pit area, or socialize in the gym bleachers, which is where all the "want to be cool" kids hung out. The top portion of the bleachers consisted of concrete and were in

Refined Silver

rows of 15 bleachers around 10 feet long. The groups of bleachers went all around the top of the gym in a connected square. On the floor level, you would find the same groupings of bleachers but made of wood and retractable so we could use the gym for P.E. during the day and basketball at night. The gym was dark in the upper bleachers while the floor level was well lit and smelled of wax floors and sweet wood mixed with a lacquered after note. My sister and I always chose the top portion of the bleachers so we could see everything and watch everyone that came in and out.

That morning, so did Ashley — Marcus' girlfriend. As my sister and I were walking up the bleachers' stairs to have a seat, she angrily stomps towards me from above and starts screaming at me, calling me a whore and a slut, then proceeds to push me. At first, I don't really respond other than to tell her I told Marcus no and that her issue is with her boyfriend and not me . Apparently, those were fight words, because she spit in my face and shoved me down the concrete bleachers . I grabbed her shirt to try to steady my feet, but it was to no avail. We both went tumbling down faster than Humpty Dumpty. Somehow, she lands on top and immediately hits me in the face.

That is the last thing I remember until Mrs. Daniels is blowing a whistle in my ear while the P.E./Wrestling Coach, the Health teacher, and my English teacher are trying to pull me off of Ashley. They get us both on our feet and I'm covered in blood. It's in my mouth, my eyes, my hair... it's everywhere. I look down at my new outfit that I had bought after working all summer long the previous summer at the greenhouse up the road. My brand new shirt is soaked in blood. It's torn and ruined. I start crying. I'm shaking, confused and now angry about my shirt. I lunge for her for round 2 but am held back by the P.E./wrestling coach. At that point, I see her face and the damage I've caused. She is being held up since she has gone limp. She looks so pale and lifeless and there is so much blood. Her eye is bulging and her cheek is gaping and exposed.

All those years of fighting for my life came out on Ashley, and even though I was defending myself, she didn't deserve my wrath in that way. They called an ambulance for her and a police officer for me. I sat in the lobby of the sheriff's office waiting for Spice to come and pick me up since the sheriff was a family friend. I sat there in now crusted bloody clothes, blood that I don't know if it belonged to her or me, and I'm now freezing and shaking. I sat there bouncing my leg, and nervously praying for God to heal her. I prayed that I didn't kill her or cause permanent damage. I pray for forgiveness. I'm not scared of what will happen to me, but I'm terrified of what is happening to her.

That day was the last day I ever allowed myself to get physical outside of a boxing ring or octagon. I still have no first-hand memory of what happened because I blacked out from the anger. From what my sister and witnesses said, when we finally landed, she was on top of me and punching me. Apparently, I wrapped my legs around her waist and grabbed her hair with my left hand while wailing away on her face with my right hand. I had split her cornea as well as ripped the corner of her right eye, fractured her jaw, split her cheek to the bone, and ripped her lip severely. She had to have surgery on her eye and her lip to repair the damage, and for years she had a lisp. I fractured two of my knuckles and had to go to the hospital and get an HIV test since they thought I had swallowed her blood since she was above me and she was known to be sexually promiscuous with boys who were also sexually promiscuous.

Those 10 minutes we fought could have forever changed our lives because of immature and wrongful actions on both of our parts. She could have killed me by pushing me down the bleachers, and I could have killed her if I had caused brain damage or hit her temple just the right way. The police charged me with assault with a deadly weapon (my hands) due to the injuries and the number of times I hit her, as well as the severity of the hits and the fact I had wrapped my legs around her, making it impossible for her to leave.

Refined Silver

We spoke 15 years ago and both apologized and forgave each other. Her lisp is gone, and her eye is OK now, but she will forever have the faint scars on her face. I will forever live with the knowledge that I could have killed her. For a brief time, I thought I did. I'm almost 40 and it still scares me to think about what I was capable of that day.

If there are any teens, reading this, please hear me, Violence is NEVER the answer unless your life is in imminent danger! You have a voice. Use your words and choose them wisely, for they cut just as deeply. I promise you, it's not worth it for you or them to fight over school drama that won't even matter after you graduate!

Off the soapbox....My life had now spiraled out of control. I was suspended, facing jail, and I was making bad decisions, surrounded by bad influences and bad men. Thankfully, God loved me too much to leave me there! He left the 99 to rescue me.

Refined Silver

For we do not wrestle against flesh and blood, but against the rulers, against the authorities, against the cosmic powers over this present darkness, against the spiritual forces of evil in the heavenly places.

Ephesians 6:12

~ 11 ~

I wasn't in trouble at home over the school fight since it was self-defense, but I also wasn't allowed to leave the property while everything was getting sorted out. Every second stuck at home was like Russian Roulette. All through winter, tensions were building and could blow at any moment. For months, money was extremely tight, and most meals consisted of leftover bagged lunches from a warehouse up the road . They would give us the bagged lunches they had left over from that day. Some days there would be 10 bags, while other days there could be 40. Every bag was the same in that it consisted of a sandwich, a hamburger or hot dog, as well as a bag of chips, a little Debbie snack cake such as Star Crunches or Zebra Cakes, and a bottle of water or soda.

What a blessing the bagged lunches were! God provided yet again, but after eating them every day for dinner, or up to 3 times a day if it was a weekend or holiday, the lunches became incredibly mundane, and as a teen, I didn't see the gift as a blessing. I longed for real meat, veggies, and fruit, as did everyone else. The electricity was turned off every month, and Spice would wait until it was turned off to scramble to get the money. It never failed that Joe would swoop in with the money to have it reconnected the next day...after Spice sent me to Nanny Emily's.

I didn't know it at the time, but she essentially sold me to Joe, Mike, or Tim (Renegade's cousin that drove down from Michigan just to prey on me). They would sexually assault me in exchange for Spice to facilitate it and look the other way. They would give her money for utilities, food, and drugs. I was pimped out or trafficked over the Tri-State area so we could have lights on and so they could buy their drugs. Lack of money also meant smaller quantities of drugs, which was a very dangerous place to be. Spice and Renegade were perpetually angry and on edge when they were running low or out of drugs.

On top of financial issues, it had been a frigid winter. The well pump had gone out the prior summer, which meant we had to draw water from the well all winter long. We would have to bundle up and go outside in the frigid cold to retrieve the water by hand from the well every time we needed water. With at least 6 people in the trailer, we always needed water. Winter that year was long and very cold, everyone's spirits were down, and our impoverished souls were tired. To give you a little perspective on what drawing water entailed, we had a 5 gallon bucket attached to a long rope. In order for the bucket to submerge into the water, we had to put a very large rock in the bucket and throw it down the well. It usually took a few tries to get the bucket at a sideways angle in order for the water to pull the bucket below the surface. When the bucket was full, we would hoist it up by hand and take it inside to boil on the stove. The water was brown from all the iron, so it didn't matter if you needed hot water or not, it had to be boiled in order to be able to use it for anything other than flushing the toilet. This was our only water source, and it had to be done several times a day. If you wanted a bath, you spent hours drawing water, boiling it in one large pot at a time, and then you would pour it into the bathtub and start another pot of water. By the 5th round, your arms were jello, so you would settle with just enough water to cover your knees, water that was now cold or room temperature at best after the length of time of drawing it up and boiling it bucket by bucket, pot by pot. If you needed to flush the toilet, you retrieved a bucket of water from the well. If you were cooking, feeding the dogs, washing clothes, or mopping the floor, you retrieved a bucket of water from the well. Since Spice and Renegade were generally too lazy or high to do it and I was the oldest, it usually fell to me to draw the water, regardless if it was for someone else or not. It's still a mystery to me as to why I didn't have arms as large as The Rock with all the heavy buckets I had to draw up. Through winter, the surface of the water in the well would freeze, which meant you spent 30 minutes having to break up the ice before you were able to drop the bucket down to get water. By the time we finished homework and started baths, it was usually dark, and it never failed, I would have to go and get water in the dark every evening, even in the snow or rain. Spoiler alert: it snows or rains in Kentucky A LOT in the winter, between the weather and sloshing water from struggling to carry a heavy bucket...you always got wet. To draw the water in the evening, I would have to hold the flashlight in my mouth because it took both hands to lift the heavy water-filled 5 gallon bucket, and I had to be able to see where the bucket landed.

The wind was the worst part of drawing water in the winter; it would whip through the trees and cut you to the bone regardless of how much you bundled up. It's the kind of wind that is cold enough for Jack Frost himself to ride in on, but he isn't just nipping at your nose. No, any sliver of skin you dare leave exposed is touched by the wind and instantly frozen. The kind of frozen that burns when you walk into a warm room, so painful yet comforting because it's so warm compared to outside but such a shock that it feels like your skin is torched by fire. Nighttime was worse as the sunshine was no longer there to warm the air even in the slightest, and you couldn't see the trees, so you couldn't brace for a stronger gust coming your way until it was already on you. We didn't own gloves, so I would take my thickest socks and layer them in hopes of keeping my fingers warm, knowing full well that it was always a bad idea. Do you know what's worse than cold hands... socks that get wet from the water and become frozen to your hands like some icicle hand mold that had to literally be peeled off your hands because the socks were so stiff.

By the time I had the ice broken up and water hauled in, my fingers would be so cold and stiff that they wouldn't bend. The small metal flashlight would be so cold that it hurt my teeth; and my jaw would be stuck in a semi-open position long after I was back in the house. Our main heat source was a kerosene heater in the middle of the living room, so every morning I would have to get up at 4 am, refill the kerosene, light the heater, draw water from the well, and boil it to wash our faces and brush our teeth. Then it was time to get my siblings up and dressed for school and then back out in the freezing cold to stand by the road in the frigid temps and watch for the bus so I could signal them to come out of the warm house and get on the cold bus.

The writing was on the wall, gasoline issues were all around us, and you could feel the rising tensions building daily as though a dark cloud loomed over our home. On Valentine's Day evening, it all came crashing down. Three of my guy friends came over to check on me and just hang out with my sister and I. Someone mentioned Chinese food (my favorite food) to celebrate the holiday and the fact that my suspension was over after the weekend. We lived in the middle of nowhere and the nearest Chinese restaurant was

30 minutes away, which meant they had to go pick the food up and leave me behind as I couldn't leave the property. Spice had been out trying to score some marijuana, leaving me at the house with our middle sister, baby brother, and Renegade.

My sister and I were in our room with the door open, giggling and gossiping while dancing to Backstreet Boys and N*Sync as we waited for our friends to arrive back with the food. I see our baby brother walking down the hall towards my room with a deck of cards in his hand. He is casually scraping the deck of cards along the wall as he walks towards me with a bored expression on his face. I know he is going to ask if we will play cards with him in our room in the hopes that he will be there when our friends get back. Suddenly, Renegade rushes towards him out of nowhere and throws my brother down the hall. Just as quickly as he charged him, Renegade jumps on him and begins punching him left and right in the back of the head. The millisecond that we went from laughing and playing to fighting for our lives was so eerily quick. It seemed like we were in this world, and then we blinked, and suddenly we were in an alternate universe of darkness and chaos.

My sister and I jump up, frantically screaming, and try to pull him off our brother. He stands up, and with one hand, lifts me slightly off the ground to where only my tiptoes are touching the floor. He slams me into the wall

Refined Silver

with such force that it leaves an indention the size of my upper body in the wall and I have to kind of peel myself out of the paneling style sheetrock. He turns his focus onto my sister and is on her lightning fast. He is continuously punching her like some enraged maniac. My brother jumps on his back and starts hitting him in the head, desperately trying to stop the assault on my sister. Renegade flips my brother off his back and proceeds to choke him. I football rush the rabid beast and knock him off my brother.

We have gone from the hall, to the living room, and now partially into the kitchen during this out of nowhere melee. The side table with the lamp and VHS tapes gets knocked over in the process. We are banging into the couches, walls, and TV stand. It's such chaos and destruction that even the Tasmanian Devil pales in comparison. All of this has progressed rapidly in a matter of a couple of minutes, yet it seemed to last a lifetime…and seemed like it was never going to end. I don't know who this person is, but he is no longer a person. He is like a rabid animal. He suddenly had herculean strength, a strength he had never displayed as ferociously in all of the previous beatings. There is no soul in his eyes, no humanity at all, just cold nothingness. By this time, my 3 friends have shown up and immediately try to help us get him off my brother again.

Refined Silver

Renegade is breathing in this carnal sound, like a deep growl that is throaty and from deep down in the soul. It mimics when a cat or dog is eating and letting others know not to come near it's prey. It's a primal growl, not like when we as humans try to imitate a lion or bear. It takes all 5 of us, but we finally get him off of my brother long enough for my brother to escape his grasp. Renegade stands up and focuses solely on me. He cocks his head to the side in such a way that it's unnatural and chilling and proceeds to charge me with such intensity and speed that it resembles a bull charging a red flag. I'm cornered with my back against the wall. I have nowhere to go, and we are all so exhausted, while Renegade isn't even winded. The fear and panic starts to creep into my mind. None of this makes sense, and I fear we are not going to make it out of this alive. In all of the commotion, we must have knocked the couch backwards, and I see my softball bat sticking out from under the couch. I grab it as he comes towards me and I ring his knee cap so strongly I can hear the grind of the metal bat against bone. He breaks out in this creepy weird laugh and begins talking to himself, but the words aren't English or any language I've ever heard, they are incoherent and unintelligible to me.

The cacophony of his creepy laugh and throaty growling mixed with my friends' shouting and freaking out, as well as my siblings' crying, is too much. I can't focus. I don't know what to do. I don't know what just happened. My hands are shaking, I'm livid, terrified and still stunned by the rapidity of it all. My cheeks begin to burn as hot tears start pouring down my face as I look around. Chinese food is now littered everywhere; lamps and VHS movies are strewn about; papers and playing cards are now mixed with broken glass. There is splattered blood everywhere.

Renegade finally goes to his bedroom, and we quickly retreat to my bedroom and lie up against the door in case he tries to come in. After a few minutes, I get my bearings back and try to convince my friends they have to leave us to go get help, as their plan was for all of us to leave and get help. We are seriously injured. All of us are bleeding, but I still don't know from where, but I do know I can't let Spice and my baby sister come back and possibly into his crosshairs. We have no way of getting a warning to them, no way to prevent this from happening to them, so I have to stay and sound the alarm when they arrive.

After some back and forth, they finally agree to leave us with the promise of sending help immediately. My jaw is throbbing and it's painful to even try to speak. Every time I move my jaw, I can hear and feel it grind. My teeth hurt all the way to the roots, to the point I reach up and touch them to make sure they aren't broken. I look over at my sister to see her face is already swelling. She is bleeding from her lip and spitting blood from an injury somewhere in her mouth.

My brother can barely speak. When he does, it's raspy and just about a whisper, partially from being choked and partially from the scene that had unfolded. He's holding the back of his head and crying from the pain. Our adrenaline slowly starts to come down and the pain from our injuries starts to register.

I don't know how long it was until Spice or the police arrived, but every second seemed to be an hour long. We sit there frozen, afraid to move, speak, or make a sound in case he tries to come into the room and attack us again. The trailer is now so quiet you can hear a pin drop. The dichotomy of the loud chaos mere minutes before and the silence now is unnerving, as though we found ourselves in a horror flick. The trees, the birds, everything around us was silent, as though nature itself witnessed what had happened and stood there just as stunned as we were. It's so quiet that I begin to question if I'm deaf and just can't hear from the assault because the world can't possibly be this quiet but still dared not make a sound to verify one way or another. My siblings and I just sit there in a daze, replaying what had just happened. As I sit there, my mind randomly recalls how hairy Renegade's arms were when he picked me up off the ground. I didn't notice it at the time, but I am strangely aware of it now. I am convinced he is a werewolf. That's the only explanation for his new found strength, the not-of-this-world throaty growling, and the lack of any humanity or light in his eyes. I start scanning

Refined Silver

the room for anything silver in case he tries to attack us again when I hear a car pull up and my baby sister's voice.

We rush out to my sister and Spice to tell them what has happened and that we need to leave immediately. All 3 of us are talking all at once, trying to explain the events, and Spice stands there confused and concerned. Until the moment I tell her the police are on their way, and then her demeanor changes instantly. She immediately starts screaming at us, that it's our fault, that we must have provoked him somehow. She screams what horrible kids we are to do this to her and how she will not let us ruin her life. She instructs us to quickly clean up all the damage in the trailer and wash our faces. We are to tell the police that we were wrestling and our friends got the wrong impression. She emphatically screams that we will NOT ruin her marriage. Spice accuses us of overreacting to the situation and causing the violence by triggering him. My jaw is off kilter and just kind of hanging like it's out of socket and every inch of my face hurts. My fractured knuckles now feel crushed and I am on the verge of throwing up. My sister's face and upper torso are already beginning to show bruises. She complains of pain in her ribs when she breathes, so I know she has some broken ribs as well. My baby brother has handprints around his throat; he is hoarse and struggles to swallow, and here she is more concerned about Renegade going to jail than our injuries that he inflicted.

Refined Silver

I am devastated and in disbelief as we try to straighten up the mess the best we can, but the evidence of it all is too much to clean up so quickly. The fried rice and sticky chicken are now smooshed into the carpet from the struggle . Broken picture frames and cracked VHS tapes litter the floor as lo mein noodles cling to the wall and are strewn over the couch. Playing cards are scattered through the hall with drops of blood all over them. The police knock on the door and Spice and Renegade start their classic dance of spinning the facts and lying their way out of what happened. The physical damage to our bodies is too great for them to excuse away. They try to arrest Renegade, but he goes berserk. It takes 3 officers and a lot of wrestling, but Renegade is finally placed in cuffs, as Spice starts screaming and pleading for the police to release him, and in the next breath, hollering at us to tell them he didn't do anything wrong, then proceeds to scream at the police again. One of the officers asks me if we need an ambulance, and Spice interjects that she will get us medical treatment after they leave before I can even respond. I know she is lying. She is going to go to a bail bondsman as soon as they leave, and we will be the enemy for weeks to come. The pain from my face is terrible, but the pain from standing there watching my mother callously lie to the police to cover up the assault is gut-wrenching.

The police have the same look of sadness and disgust in their eyes as I do, as if they can read my thoughts. One of the deputies tells her if she bails Renegade out, he cannot come back here. This isn't his first time here, or second, or third. He knows Renegade will be back here before nightfall, as he has been every time before. As one of the male deputies takes my statement, I tell him I'm afraid for us to be left alone with her because she is spiraling into a manic episode and thinks this is all our fault, which means we will be her targets of wrath. I ask if we can go with them, because I am truly scared. I have never seen her this frantic before, and we are severely hurt. The deputy calls Nanny Emily and instructs Spice to take us to her house immediately, and then they were gone, with the possessed Renegade in the back seat grinning ear to ear. We go back inside to get some clothes and the trailer seems hollow. The remaining remnants of the events prior are still scattered about, but it is so different than how it was earlier, it almost seems like we imagined it.

Before we can close the door, Spice screams in my face that she hates us, accuses us of doing it on purpose because we never wanted to see her happy and that she wishes she had never given birth to us. My siblings are crying, partially from fear as Spice has become unhinged and partially because she isn't concerned about us at all. As we stand there battered and bruised, all she speaks of is how this is unfair to Renegade and how she's convinced it's our sole mission to ruin her life. After an hour of this, I begin to doubt whether she is really going to drop us off at Nanny

Refined Silver

Emily's house. I start trying to form a plan in my head on how we can get help because we don't have any way to call the police or Nanny Emily. We need treatment for our injuries as they are too severe for some Tylenol and Band-Aids. I have never been in fear of my life from Spice before, so I don't know how far she is willing to go in her downward spiral.

Out of the blue, she tells us to get into the car, and since we want to go to Nanny Emily's so badly, we can be Nanny Emily's problem from now on. She tells us she is washing her hands of us and that we are dead to her. Her words cut us to the core. Seeing the heartbreak in my siblings' eyes is my undoing. I'm filled with anger at the audacity of Spice and heartbroken that she can't be a supportive and loving mother for my siblings. I'm disgusted that Renegade has this strong of a hold on her that she is unwavering in her loyalty to him versus us children.

In the car, we have minutes of silently crying followed by minutes of her belligerently screaming. Rinse and repeat the entire way. All the while, she is speeding down the winding road. We see a gas truck driving slowly up ahead, far slower than we are going. She isn't slowing down: her foot never comes off the pedal. Trees are whipping by us as I tell her to slow down. All of the kids are just as frantic as I am. They are begging and crying for her to slow down because she is going to wreck. My middle sister tries to speak sense into her, but it's going in one ear and out the other. She is in her own head and her own pain, oblivious to anything we say.

We are close to slamming into the truck when Spice tells us that she should intentionally hit the truck and kill us all. She starts accelerating as I start praying out loud, begging God to save us. I know she is about to kill us all. Mere feet from the truck, it swerves into a field to avoid us.

Everything after that is a blur until we finally arrive at Nanny Emily's and all of us kids rush out of the suicide car before it's too late. Nanny Emily comes running out to us. Even in the shadows of the night and porch light, she can see the severity of our injuries and exclaims in horror that we look like we fought a demon. I run to her and collapse in her arms as I reply…"We did."

Refined Silver

From oppression and violence he redeems their life,
and precious is their blood in his sight.

Psalms 72:14

~ 12 ~

We spent the night at the hospital having bones mended and skin stitched, but even with all the doctors and nurses we saw that night, no one could fix our broken hearts or erase the sheer terror that we had experienced. Something forever changed in us. My middle sister, baby brother and I were bonded in a way we never knew before. We had experienced and fought true evil and survived. However, the experience left us unable to even put words to it. How do you describe what only your spirit can feel? How do you describe the righteous anger and disgust from the depths of your soul as though it's from the marrow of your body? An unknown place and depth, as though this secret place is grafted into you that you were unaware of until you felt it revolting and retching just from being in the presence of such evil?

You can't, or at least I can't. I have yet to find the right words or combination of words to describe what only the Holy Spirit can. All the words in all the languages fail to truly capture what it feels like when you are locked in with a demon and fighting for your life. Even as you read about what happened that night, I know I have failed as an author to accurately put into words any description or portrayal that even comes close to accurately describing what we experienced. It wasn't until I sat in a Theology class a couple of years ago and learned about demon possession that I completely let go of my werewolf theory. However, if the Winchesters ever get back together, call me...I'm just saying, I have had werewolf/demon hunting experience.

Spice was calm by the next morning, which we knew meant she had already bailed Renegade out of jail. For a couple of days, she kept up the charade that she hadn't bailed him out and she was leaving him for good. We had heard that line countless times before and knew it was an empty promise, a translucent lie. She did keep the lie going for a bit until one evening, when she picked up my baby sister and took her to the house for a couple of hours, and my sister unintentionally exposed the truth. When she came back that evening, she started telling us what she had done, what she had eaten, etc. In the process of relaying the events, she accidentally let it slip that Renegade was at the house while my baby sister was there.

The judge had made it clear that should Renegade acquire bail, he was not allowed to have any contact with any of us. Nanny Emily used this newfound knowledge as leverage against Spice to ensure that we did whatever Nanny Emily wanted. For a couple of months, we went back and forth between Nanny Emily and Spice. Spice made sure Renegade wasn't around when we went over, with the exception of being when my baby sister would go by herself. Since she wasn't there that night, she didn't see him as the monster that we did. She enjoyed spending time with him and was convinced it was just an awful mistake that would never happen again. It fractured our relationship with her because she loved him and she defended him out of loyalty. We constantly felt as though we had to convince her of the evil that we experienced that night, yet she so easily took Spice and Renegade at their word. It was baffling to me.

I didn't understand how Spice was under his spell and now so was my baby sister. I had experienced domestic violence first-hand my whole life, but as a teenager I didn't understand the mentality domestic violence victims have regarding their abusers. My heart hurts for my baby sister as I look back and think of what a tough position all of us put her in. She was pulled between us and them; siblings vs. parents; a war where both sides would cheat to be the winner, and both sides wanted her to be their spy.

During those months, our home life wasn't the only thing changing. Nanny Emily immediately forced me to break up with my drug-transporting boyfriend. My sister and I were no longer allowed to go out with friends. Listening to rap or hip hop was forbidden, as was being on the phone after 9 pm on school nights. Nanny Emily doled out these new rules to hold us accountable, to ensure we were safe, and to help us make smart decisions. Spice would enforce them when she was mad at us, but in the next breath, give us permission to do it when she was mad at Nanny Emily. We were constantly in a state of uncertainty. You dare not say, "Well, I'm allowed to do this at Nanny's house," or vice versa, as it would ignite WW3, not just for you, but between Spice and Nanny Emily as well. You never truly knew what was allowed or who was in charge. Spice said it didn't matter what Nanny Emily said because she was the boss, and Nanny Emily would say she was in charge and that Spice no longer had a say. It was a constant battle of tug of war that created instability. Spice would still let me go out with friends or listen to rap, but I couldn't wear makeup to school. While at Nanny Emily's, I wasn't allowed to go out, but I could wear makeup to school. You had two sets of rules and it became increasingly confusing, especially when you didn't know whose house you would be at that day or who was calling the shots. It became so hard to keep up that my friends and I came up with a system to skirt certain rules so we didn't get in trouble regardless of where I was. As a teenager, all I cared about was talking on the phone, so my friends and I came up with a way to talk on the phone without getting caught. Back then, you could call "time and temperature" by dialing a local number and an automated voice would tell you the current time and temperature as well as the projected forecast. After it went through its 30 second, pre-recorded automated message, it would automatically disconnect. Since I wasn't allowed on the phone after 9 pm, my friends would be told to call at 9:10 exactly or whatever time we came up with that day. I would then sneak one of the cordless phones into the bathroom at 9:08 pm and call time and temperature every 30 seconds until I heard a call beeping in, then I would switch over and talk. This sneaky ploy kept the phone from ringing and allowed me to talk as long as I wanted. I would spend the next couple of hours whispering into the phone while still listening to hear if anyone was coming. If I did hear someone coming to use the bathroom, I would quickly drop the phone in the dirty clothes hamper and flush the toilet to pretend I had been using the bathroom. The number of times my friends heard others using the bathroom while they waited patiently in the hamper for me to come back will forever give me immature childlike comedy.

I digress. Court was finally scheduled for sentencing of Renegade/custody of us siblings all in one hearing. The plan was for Nanny Emily to get custody of us and hopefully force Spice to leave Renegade in order for her to regain custody. We were supposed to stand before the judge, with Spice and everyone else watching and tell the judge who we wanted to live with. The painful position you are in as a child in the courtroom, there to choose which parent you prefer while both of them stare at you, is unfair and heartbreaking because you don't want to hurt either parent or let them down. Regardless of what has happened, there is a natural love and protectiveness that is directly opposed to the logical aspect of knowing they are not the safest and most stable place for you. The guilt of betrayal makes you question your own logic. "Maybe this time, she will finally leave him. Maybe he has changed and will never do it again. Maybe we can finally be a big happy family."

You know that nothing will ever change and that these are all imaginary fealties, but you so desperately want it to be so that you almost convince yourself. I didn't want to live with Nanny Emily, but I didn't want to go back to foster care ever again. Outside of the Millers, foster care was always the loneliest part of my childhood, where the majority of my time was spent isolated or in tears. Foster care also meant I would be separated from my siblings because four is too many for most people. We were finally all together, and I didn't want to lose them again. I had three options, which not only affected me, but more importantly, they affected my siblings. Option one: we all live with Nanny Emily in her small two-bedroom house and in Joe's crosshairs. Option two: go into foster care where you can't work or drive and will most likely be split up into different homes. Option three: return to the holler with Spice and Renegade, where there are few basic necessities; but plenty of drugs, predators, and abuse.

Refined Silver

After much discussion, the four of us siblings agreed that Nanny Emily's was the best option. The plan was for all four of us to tell the judge that we wanted to live with Nanny Emily. We would share a room until they bought a bigger place and never be alone in any room or place on the property for safety from Joe. We walked into the courthouse that morning. I was so nervous that my skinny knees would click into each other and I was afraid others would hear them trembling and knocking into each other. I walked in knowing that no matter what happened, when we walked out today, our family would forever be broken. Hearts would be shattered, hard lines drawn in the sand, but most of all, I walked in knowing… there would be no winners. What I didn't know was Goliath's brother (Mark), sister (Beatrice), and mother (Nanny Evelyn), all from North Carolina, would be sitting on one of the wooden benches. Apparently, Nanny Emily and I were the only ones who didn't know, because my siblings ran over to them and began talking in a way that was clear this was not a "first conversation in a long time" exchange. We proceeded into court, and it seemed that even the judge wasn't surprised that they were there. All the preparation and courage I had mustered up was now wiped away with confusion and surprise. We were 10-15 minutes into the proceeding before I realized I had zoned out and had no idea what had been said. The judge said in exchange for Renegade getting a reduced sentence of community service, Spice had relinquished all parental rights. The sheer pain that pierced my soul with just one sentence was so great it caused my knees to buckle and I fell to the ground. My baby sister and I began to cry. The silent tears fell down our faces as though our souls themselves were weeping.

I still had not put two and two together until Uncle Mark stepped up to the podium and requested custody of my baby brother. The judge asked my brother if he would like that, and my brother immediately agreed. Before a breath was even taken, the judge said "So ordered". I couldn't even begin to comprehend what had just happened. Next up, Aunt Beatrice and Nanny Evelyn stepped up to the podium and requested custody of my two sisters, they agreed and the judge immediately said "so ordered" again. Nanny Emily was awarded temporary custody of me and court was adjourned. All in the span of five minutes, my family was forever split up and I had zero say in any of it. We gave each other a long hug in the parking lot of the courthouse, with the adults promising us that we would get to see each other every year and talk on the phone often. Then off to our new homes we went. Visiting each other never happened, and only one phone call ever took place.

I went back to Nanny Emily's, in a haze. I'm stunned, devastated beyond belief, and scared for them and for me. How can we look out for one another if we are states away from each other? I'm now all alone, living 24/7 in a house with Joe. I am too afraid to even shower or bathe naked, so I wear panties and shorts into the shower and wash like usual, but with clothes on. After I am done bathing, I quickly take off my wet panties and shorts, rush through drying off, and then put on my clean clothes before ever stepping out of the tub. I never wash my hair while in the shower for fear of not being able to see with the soapy water running over my face, thus making me exposed and vulnerable. So, after I showered, I would have Nanny Emily wash my hair in the kitchen sink under the guise that I couldn't do it properly.

My bedroom is the laundry room with a bed in the corner. There is no door, just a washer and dryer and me… exposed while I sleep, even more so since his bedroom is next to mine. Nanny Emily had slept on a couch for as long as I could remember and never once slept in the bed with Joe. She always claimed she had horrendous pain in her legs and arms and would sleep on the couch so she could prop up whichever limb was hurting her by throwing it over the arm of the sofa or back of the couch. I couldn't sleep in my bed for fear of being sexually assaulted, so I slept on the loveseat beside her, knowing Joe wouldn't be brazen enough to try something while I slept next to her.

My siblings never told me that they had been talking to Uncle Mark and the others that whole time, which left me feeling betrayed and alone. They never told me that Aunt

Beatrice and Uncle Mark bribed them with four-wheelers, toys, and opportunities if they would move down there with them. They never told me they had it all figured out weeks before we ever went to court…. they never told me they were leaving me. I couldn't cry about it in front of Nanny Emily for fear of her becoming angry at me for missing them. The moment my siblings chose to go with Goliath's family was the moment they became dead to her. I wasn't allowed to take up for them, cry for them, or even speak of them because she always said, "you don't talk to dead people."

My best friend Nathan was there the night Renegade attacked us. He had been there with me for court and was one of the only two friends that was still by my side. When I was heartbroken over my siblings, he was the only person I could cry to. I had known he had a crush on me for years, but it wasn't until that season that I began to see him as more than a friend.

I had worked all summer long in order to get out of the house and away from Joe as often as I could. When I wasn't working at the greenhouse or the summer program at school, I was doing an internship for Physical Therapy as part of my duel enrollment for college and high school.

School was about to begin and I had finally had some semblance of a normal teenage life, outside of Joe, of course.

I didn't want for anything, I always had a home cooked meal, and had just been accepted to the University of Kentucky, Shawnee State University, Ohio State, and several others. To celebrate the success and turnaround in my life that summer, Nanny Emily let me go to the fair with Nathan and his mom with the caveat that I would bring her back a candy apple. I had never been to a fair before and was completely enthralled with everything from the lights to the food, the rides, even the smell of the air that night. Sitting atop the Ferris wheel, looking out over the city lights, was the most magical thing I had ever seen. I rode the most exhilarating, heart-stopping roller coasters, boat rides, and even one where you were strapped to a vest and taken 40 feet in the air and then dropped like you were going to hit the ground. Just when you thought it was too late (I'm sure it was still 20 feet off the ground even though it seemed like 20 inches), you suddenly found yourself swinging back and forth like an out of control pendulum.

Once I realized I was indeed still alive and not a splattered body on the ground, I closed my eyes, the wind whipping in my hair, and for a moment, it felt like I was flying. For the first time in so long, if ever, soaring through the air, I felt free. We stayed until they closed the last ride down, arms full of stuffed animals, balloons, and memories of a lifetime, and we drove back to Nanny Emily's, without her candy apple. I realized my mistake about halfway home, and I knew I would be in massive trouble. We stopped by the grocery store and I bought a bag of apples, a candy apple kit, and popsicle sticks in hopes that I would be forgiven if I made her a whole bag of apples as an apology. When I got home, I immediately "fessed" up to my mistake, and apologized profusely. I explained that I would stay up all night making her candy apples and I would never forget again.

Nothing I said mattered after "I forgot your candy apple." She accused me of being like Spice and only concerned with boys. She told me I was selfish and after all she did for me, how dare I treat her like this? She hollered and degraded me for several hours until she finally sent me to my room in tears. The next morning, I woke up to all my clothes in trash bags by the front door. She told me she would not go through with raising a spoiled teenager again (like she did with Spice) and that I could no longer live there. I had one hour to find someone to come and get me or she would call child protective services and have them take me. Of all the people I called, no one answered except for a 25-year-old man that I knew from working at the green-house. He was a fiber optic specialist and told me I could live at his house since he was rarely there. He picked me up, and by lunch time, I was living alone in a borrowed house with a man 10 years older than me who I barely knew. I lost the last family I had, the last person who was supposed to inherently love me… all over a candy apple.

Refined Silver

He dropped me off at his house and left town for work within the first couple of hours. Here I was all alone at his bachelor pad of a house, and almost immediately had a gut feeling that this was a mistake. Regardless, there was no putting the genie back in the bottle. My family on both sides didn't want me, just like the Millers had not wanted me. Why was I so hard to love? I couldn't believe my life had all come to this, because I had forgotten a candy apple. On the one hand, I never had to worry about Joe, Renegade, or Goliath ever again. On the other hand, I now had to worry about how I was going to survive on my own… all the while still in high school.

Refined Silver

You restored me to health and let me live. Surely it was for my benefit that I suffered such anguish. In your love you kept me from the pit of destruction; you have put all my sins behind your back.

Isaiah 38:16-17

~ 13 ~

Living alone with some random guy, albeit as nice as he was, was not a good idea, so after just a week there, Nathan's parents let me stay with them for the weekend until we could figure out what to do. Nathan's dad was against it once I got there though, so much so that he had me go to bed at 8 pm and I was not allowed to get up until another adult was awake the next morning. To ensure that hormonal teenagers weren't stupid and sneaky, he placed his recliner in front of my bedroom door and slept in it. After the weekend, it was clear that this was not a viable solution either. So I filed for emancipation (essentially, where the court allows you to make decisions for yourself as though you are an adult even though you are still a minor). I already had a job, great grades, multiple college acceptance letters, wonderful character references, as well as a place of my own since Nathan's parents would give me a trailer to live in that was on their property if I was emancipated.

We were all certain the judge would grant the emancipation and had already started renovating the trailer. Plot twist... he didn't. Instead, he makes me a ward of the state, which means foster care until I'm 18. Because of my arrest from the school fight, my foster home was the one where they sent juvenile delinquents to stay. I'm taken to Jack and Bea's home, an elderly couple who were more rigid than the military and meaner than junkyard dogs. As soon as I arrive, I am immediately sent to my room, which is in the center of the house, as though someone built a dungeon room and then built a house around it. There are no windows, there isn't a TV, radio, lamp, nada. Just 4 sets of bunk beds, a dresser of 9 drawers with a mirror, spread around a large square room with a padlock on the door.

I'm greeted by a pregnant 16-year-old backwoods country girl, who is going to be my cell mate, aka my roommate. She confides in me that night that she is running away the next day and she and her baby daddy are going to get married and live happily ever after. Yet, in the next breath, she requests my help to correctly spell even small words as she writes her letter of intent to whom I assume to be child services.

I lay in bed crying myself to sleep. How did I get here? How am I in the same place as the pregnant teen, who stole a car and went joyriding with her boyfriend, and who obviously has skipped school many times? I am a good kid. Yes, I made some mistakes, but I have a good heart. I'm kind, forgiving, and helpful. I don't understand why I'm so hard to love.

Refined Silver

The next day, she runs away from school and I never see her again. There's no one to share a room with anymore... it's just me. I don't know if they caught her, I don't know if she got her happily ever after, but I do know she never came back to Jack and Bea's. I had been in foster care several times before, and there were fleeting moments when I thought of running away. Yet, I couldn't understand how being pregnant and homeless was better than living with Jack and Bea... until I lived with them. It wasn't long until I understood why the illiterate, impoverished country bumpkin would risk it all for freedom. During the school year, I get up in the morning, get dressed, and ride the bus to school. In the afternoons, the bus drops me off and I have to go straight to my room where they lock me in with a padlock. If I need to use the bathroom, I have to knock and wait until they aren't too busy to let me out. I have to stay in the room until the next morning, only to be let out for school minus a quick dinner, a 10 minute shower, or attending church services with them.

I had always been raised in southern Baptist churches. Jack and Bea were Pentecostal, naïve me thought church was church. So, when I first arrive and they tell me we have to attend church every week, I innocently reply, " How different can Pentecostal be as opposed to Southern Baptist?" Let me tell you a little secret... it was a very different experience. At the southern Baptist churches I attended, you sang two songs from a hymn book that the preacher's wife chose while she played the hymns on her piano, which was the only musical instrument we had. I always thought two songs at our church were plenty for worshipping God, because, bless their hearts, the cacophony of noise from the two songs sounded like the opposite of worship. The pastor's wife would bang out the notes on a piano that was well past the need for tuning, but it didn't matter because no one sang on key. The pastor would stand at the podium singing monotone mixed in with the occasional loud squeal from the microphone (which was technology's way of telling us we didn't need to amplify the chaos.)

Mrs. Barbara would be one of the loudest, yet the one that was most off key. I'm positive she just created her own notes. Then you had Mrs. Margaret who must have been auditioning for the opera. I was convinced the chandeliers and stained glass windows were going to crack at any moment. Now you add in Mr. Tom, who is behind and still singing verse one while we were already ending the chorus part. Then you add a couple gifted singers, which further highlights the rest of the congregation's failed attempts. As if that wasn't enough, you sprinkle in the ventriloquist mumblers, the ones that are moving their mouths but no sound is coming out except for the occasional robustly loud word. Mmmm mmm mmmmm LORD hmmm mmmmm SAVED mmmhmm mhhmmm ME.

Refined Silver

Trust me.......two songs were more than enough. After that, you prayed, then you sat down and listened to the sermon...quietly. Then you had an altar call, another hymn, a prayer and done.

We didn't have drums, food, or drinks in the sanctuary. Missing communion was a cardinal sin, and we didn't have shouting or speaking in church . We most definitely didn't talk about the Holy Spirit either. He was the crazy uncle that no one claimed. He was the Encanto's Bruno of the Godhead trio . *Cue We don't talk about Bruno, no no no song from Encanto". You didn't say Amen except at the end of prayer and then only the men could say it aloud, you dared not dance or move. You were to be quiet and calm at all times. How different could a Pentecostal church be? (Yes, I hear your laughter from here. I learned real fast....it was in fact VERY different.)

The first night, I went to their Pentecostal church with them. I walk into this particularly beautiful white brick church and it doesn't look any different. The pews are wooden lacquered pews sitting atop burgundy carpet. There are flowers in the windows and a large wooden podium, centered on a platform at the front of the pews. I walk in thinking it's not that different. Two hours later, I walk out unsure I am going to survive... literally. I can't decide if they are possessed or crazier than a square-wheeled bicycle. Either way, I was ready to be locked away.

Refined Silver

I don't know if this particular church was different from other Pentecostal churches, but let me paint a picture of my experience at Jack and Bea's church.

We are not even one complete song in and yet, a couple of the women jump up and start screaming and chanting words that sound like gibberish. I immediately hit the floor, because I think there is a serial killer in the building with the levels of screaming that is now happening. It is a shock to my southern Baptist sense, to say the least. It only gets crazier by the second song, when a woman behind me suddenly starts running up and down the aisle with her arms flailing in the air like she is on fire. Then a man falls down and starts chanting as he is flopping around on the floor, mimicking a fish out of water. Everywhere I look, people are running or jumping and all of them are speaking different language that sounds like chanting. I begin searching for exits and waiting for everyone to start running toward them, there must be a fire or chemical spill, and we are all in danger. Get out people, save yourself!!! My eyes are the size of saucers as no one is moving outside of acting like they are burning alive. Just then, a middle-aged man comes behind me and places his hand on my head and starts chanting and shaking my head as the weight of it is bending my knees. I ask Bea what is going on as she is just clapping and singing, completely unfazed by the theatrics of it all. She tells me they "caught the Holy Spirit," as though he were an infectious disease that makes you delirious or worse—tricks you into thinking you were literally on fire. I didn't know how you "caught the Holy Spirit", but I knew I didn't want to catch him or worse, let him catch me. So the only logical thing to do was hold my breath the entire service, except for a quick inhale and exhale of breath periodically.

The next day, I called my social worker and unsuccessfully beg her not to make me go back to church with them and to schedule a doctor's appointment to see if I "caught the Holy Spirit." Thankfully, Nathan's grandmother was in charge of the neighboring Child Service's department and she pulled some strings for me. I could stay with my best friend Claire on Friday and Saturday nights and go to their Baptist church with Nathan and his family on Sunday. Afterwards, they would drop me off for my life of solitude until the next Friday.

There isn't a lamp, TV, or any other source of light minus the overhead ceiling fan/light. So I would leave it on while I slept so as to not sleep in the dark. After the first night, Jack and Bea put a stop to that as "it's a waste of electricity" and "you don't need lights when you close your eyes." I have been afraid of the dark ever since I could remember. (I still am at almost 40-years-old). I'm am waiting for the day Motel 6 asks me to be a spokesperson since "we'll leave the light on for you" is a mantra in my house. I digress, the crossbow incident and men trying to rape me in my sleep didn't help with that fear either. So, Claire gives me a small lamp, but Jack and Bea won't let me use it either, as it is a waste of electricity. The lights have to be off by 9:30 and to ensure it is pitch black, they start removing the light bulbs from the overhead light at bedtime. It's so dark, there is nothing for my eyes to even adjust to. I can't even make out my hand when I hold it up to my face.

Within minutes, my heart is racing and I'm struggling to breathe. My clammy hands are shaking. I'm too afraid to lie down and expose myself even more, so I curl up with my back against the wall while hugging my legs. I begin to cry. My body begins to shake so badly that it seems that even my insides are quivering from fear, until I fall asleep late into the morning hours, frequently waking up covered in sweat and overcome with fear that Joe or one of the other men who raped me was in my room. I sneak a small square light blue night light in my backpack and make sure to take it to school with me so not to get caught. It doesn't cast off much light, so that it isn't seen through any cracks under the door. It's so dim that the blue barely cascades onto my pillow beside it; I can't even see any words as I try to write in my journal. Yet, it's something, like in life, even the smallest light, the smallest of hope can break through the darkness. For hours each night, I sit alone with no one to talk to, nothing to do, just sit and think... in the dark. I'm in the worst of my nightmares. I'm in foster care and in a home where I'm not wanted. I'm all alone with no one to talk to, and even worse, I'm stuck in the dark most of the time.

The charges are thankfully dropped when school footage and witnesses confirm it was self- defense, but since I am a ward of the state, I'm still required to take anger management classes. I go to therapy where the therapist opens wounds and scars and then sends me home to sit by myself and try to cauterize the bleeding wounds. Why am I unlovable? Why does no one want me? Maybe I deserved it all? I look in the mirror and gaze into my own eyes. I talk to my reflection as though it is someone in the room with me and try to speak reason to my heart. I have been deserted by everyone I have ever loved. I am now a prisoner, literally locked away 5 days a week and consumed with so much pain, it has snuffed out any joy. I see the raw pain and devastation in my own golden-green-brown crying eyes for the first time.

After months of this, my willpower is gone. I have convinced myself that I am unlovable, unworthy and unwanted. It doesn't matter that I have sung for 2 presidents; it doesn't matter that I am a good student or have received a Presidential Achievement award; it doesn't matter that I have friends, a boyfriend or supportive teachers. The pain is so immense that it consumes every crevice of my soul. I no longer recognize the girl in the mirror. Instead I see a broken, frail, ugly girl who has been abused, stabbed, raped, beat on and discarded like trash. I am unworthy and can't even love myself. Every evening at dinner, Jack and Bea saw the same little broken girl and would make sure to tell me so. Jack was always the most harsh, he had a gruff voice that was clipped with superiority. Being in his early 60s, he had declared himself a master of people and lived by the philosophy that the stock you were born into was indicative of who you were or would be. They both had access to my case file and weaponized it to inflict pain. Either I was going to be just like my biological parents and marry an abuser or become addicted to drugs or alcohol, or that I would never amount to anything because I never had someone teach me how to be a normal person. They would often remark how no one wanted me and I should grovel and thank them for taking in an orphan like me. They would say that the state barely paid them for me, so their taking me in was an act of charity. They acted as though they were saints, and I should declare such on command.

As to make me aware of my status or lack thereof, when I received clothing vouchers from the state, Bea would only let me shop at Goodwill because I was a charity, so I needed to shop at charity stores. One day, while Bea was cooking, she let me out of my room to come help her in the kitchen. She lays out several cast iron skillets of different sizes and wants me to show her which one resembled the cast iron skillet that Goliath used to break off a piece of my skull when he beat me in the head with a cast iron skillet when I was 10 years old. From that point on, that was the skillet she used to cook dinner each night and the skillet I had to wash every night when I cleaned the kitchen. Jack had read in my file about the time Goliath had stabbed me in the ribs and instructed me to show him my scar to prove it actually happened. I told him that it was just below my left breast so I couldn't show him, in which he chastised me for using the word breast and had me go into the bathroom and show Bea to prove the scar existed. They never threatened me directly or physically abused me, but their words and the thinly veiled innuendoes left me walking on eggshells when I was allowed out of my room.

Thankfully, two days a week, I was able to be a normal teenager. Claire and I would stay up super late gossiping and laughing, or go mudding with her sister and sister's boyfriend while we jammed out to C.C.R. I would watch lifetime movies with her mom while we vegged out on takeout every Friday night. I was able to go on dates with Nathan and to school dances or football games. For 2 days a week, I was free and had just enough joy and love to make it all the more painful when I was back at Jack and Bea's. The dichotomy of the two lives was so different; it would feel as though I was living two different lives. Come Sunday after church, the feeling of heartache and dread would start mounting for the dreaded 2 p.m. drop off at Jack and Bea's.

Originally, going to church was just an excuse not to go back to the Bruno church and to have some semblance of freedom, but Revival came around and it changed everything. I walked into the church that evening, and something deep down inside of me was energized. My soul was fluttering like a kaleidoscope of butterflies. I sit in my usual pew and the emotions and joy are surreal. We do our usual songs, and my spirit is just jovial and singing along. Then the guest pastor starts preaching, and every few minutes, my butt starts scooting up further to the edge of my seat. By altar call, my butt was practically off the seat, just sitting on air. The pastor's wife starts playing "Jesus is tenderly calling," and I run to the altar. I fall to my knees and my spirit is crying out. I have been saved and baptized since I was a little girl, but this night, I knew that girl was gone and I was broken. I needed Jesus to redeem me, this older, broken version of me. I needed Jesus. I needed to sit in God's presence. I needed the Holy Spirit to walk with me. I poured out my soul that night.

The carpet around my knees became wet from the tears, my body trembled as I asked for forgiveness and redemption. I went through every instance of pain, every mistake, every hurt, every sin there on my knees. The guest pastor and home pastor kneel on either side of me, they put their hands on each of my shoulders and they pray for me and with me. The congregation comes up in droves until they are all on their knees praying alongside of me. Everyone is in tears, the Holy Spirit is roaring through each of us, and it's all directed to God on my behalf. I hear each of their whispered prayers in my ears, but I can't decipher what they say, as I am in the presence of my Father. That night, the altar on which I sang, the altar I walked by weekly, was no longer just a wooden and carpeted altar. It was a portal. I didn't run to the altar... I ran to my Father, and there he was waiting for me with open arms.

After 40 minutes, we stood up, and it's evident that everyone had been crying. The carpet is now a puddle, visible to the naked eye. I re-dedicated my life to Christ, I surrendered it all to God and I prayed to "catch the Holy Spirit" and I'm happy to report, he is my best friend! I was baptized again when I re-dedicated myself to Christ.

Because my spirit is so big, I always joke... I had to be double dipped. I walked out that night understanding the excitement and exhilaration I had witnessed at Jack and Bea's Pentecostal church. I was so excited and happy that I could have done backflips all the way down the aisle of the church. My body wasn't on fire, but the Holy Spirit sure did set my soul on fire!

Refined Silver

Many are the plans in a person's heart,
but it is the Lord's purpose that prevails.

Proverbs 19:21

Refined Silver

~ 14 ~

I spent the next year and a half living my separate lives, the imprisoned life and the normal teenage life, but my outlook was different after that revival night. Jack and Bea's teenage granddaughter moved in across from my dungeon, aka my bedroom. She was my age but had everything I didn't. She made it her mission to make it painfully obvious any chance she got. They let her go out for sports; she shopped at the mall, went to tanning beds, had satellite TV and was allowed to listen to music. Her door was never locked, she didn't have a curfew or bedtime, and it was clear she could speak to me however she wanted with zero consequences. She was so mean and rude and the very epitome of a spoiled brat. She had moved in because her mother, Jack and Bea's biological daughter had robbed a gas station.

She wore skimpy clothes, frequently fought with Jack and Bea, and slammed her door while blaring music that rattled the walls. Yet I was the problem. Once she moved in, the emotional and verbal abuse between the three of them was relentless. I desperately needed a haircut and often asked to get one and was promptly told no every time. Yet she had her hair done every 6 weeks. Bea would force me to go and sit for five hours at the salon and watch her get her hair done. Thankfully, Claire's older sister was skilled with scissors and started cutting my hair for me when I needed it. It wasn't perfect, but it was better than not having a haircut at all, and we always had such a blast laughing and being silly in the process. In a way, Claire and her family were the family I wish I had. In a way, they were my family. They accepted me, helped me, loved me, and always included me. I know I must have been in the way at least some of the time, but they never made me feel like an imposition. Nathan's parents bought me a Bible and a bookmark light shortly after my re-dedication. Every time Jack, Bea, or their granddaughter hurt my feelings, every time they tore me down, every time I was sad or lonely, I would read my Bible. I would read it before bed with my little bookmark light and before school in the mornings. Every day, my spirit grew and the pain was less than the day before.

I was still in therapy, and then spent the entire week locked in my room. Let me tell you, God transformed my room. It was no longer a room of solitude; instead, he transformed it into a healing room. There, God, Jesus, and the Holy Spirit were healing me as I spent daily time with the Holy Spirit and God's word. There in the solitude, God healed, restored, and redeemed.

He taught me forgiveness, empathy, sympathy, joy, and, above all, peace and worth. All those years of being mistreated and torn down, God picked up the pieces and built me up better than before because I had finally surrendered it all to him.

I always had to prove my worth to my family or my foster parents. I had to earn their approval by acts of work, accomplishments, and accolades, only to find it fleeting once the moment had passed. But God didn't want my works; he wanted my heart. He didn't want the perfect me, he wanted the broken, imperfect me. Even though I was still a prisoner 5 days a week, Christ had freed me, and my soul soared like an eagle released from captivity. In that room, he freed me from the consequence of eternal death and separation from God. He also freed me from the chains of generational cycles of addiction, abuse, and unhealthy relationships; chains that will never have a hold on me and therefore won't imprison my children. That is what my God did and still does. He is good, faithful, everlasting, and he called me by name! He took a discarded orphan girl, gave me robes of white, a crown, adopted me into his family, and poured out an abundance of grace, mercy, and love. All the lies of the enemy, all the weight of others' sins that weighed on my heart, he erased them all, and he wrote his image of me on my heart. He called me holy, beloved, cherished, worthy, and HIS.

Being locked away for two years was one of the greatest gifts I could have ever received because it was two years of therapy with God as he was crafting me to be a healthy,

Refined Silver

loving servant after his own heart. Two years of uninterrupted time with my Father, where he showed me the long and arduous search and rescue he did for me... and for you. He didn't judge me on his throne; he sat me on his lap, answered every question, assured every doubt, and taught me what unconditional love looked like.

With all that healing and restoration, I would love to say that I learned how to be perfect, never making a foolish mistake again... but I would be lying. As with all of us, the lies of the enemy and our flesh, coupled with living in a broken world — it doesn't take much fear of the future or lack of provisions to convince us that we have to fix our problems ourselves. Instead of giving it to God. Instead of being faithful and still, patiently waiting for him to solve our problems, we rush out to fix them ourselves out of fear and impatience.

I was turning 18 in just a few short months when I learned that the day you turn 18, you're out. No support system, no money or furnishings, no housing, no family, just you against the world completely unprepared. The reality hit harder each day I came closer to turning 18. My very first day as an adult was also going to be my very first day homeless as an adult. Claire had moved away to college, so weekends at her house were fewer and fewer. She ended up getting pregnant, dropping out of college, and moving back in with her parents. Moving in with them when I turned 18 was not an option, and I had nowhere else to turn to. I had no money for a car, car insurance, food, or rent and couldn't even afford to finish the one semester I had left for my two-year degree in Music Appreciation Arts and a secondary degree in Language Arts. Nathan asked his parents if they would be willing to let me have the trailer that they had offered years before, and they said yes, on one condition: we get married.

I didn't love Nathan like that. He was my boyfriend for several years, but I never thought he was the dreamiest man in the world. He never made my heart skip a beat, but he was one of the few steady presences through those 3 years of pain. I knew he wasn't the man I had dreamt of often when I was younger. The man in my dreams was strong, tan, with dark hair, and was a warrior. Nathan was none of that, so I did the only logical thing my 18-year-old self could think to do... I got married.

The day I turned 18, I awoke to find all of my belongings thrown into the dreaded black trash bags and sitting on the front porch . Jack and Bea told me I was a fool and would end up just like my parents, amounting to nothing. They shut the door and closed that chapter of my life before I ever stepped off the porch. I stepped off the steps full of ambition to make this a success and stood there for a moment in the blazing July sun, prickling my face with the hot rays as I let them warm my bones. It was rare that I got to experience the sun on a weekday. It had been so long and I soaked it all in. Happy 18th birthday to me.

The next day, I stood in the basement of the church, looking at myself in the mirror, standing there in my wedding gown with a sinking pit in my gut.

The Holy Spirit had been telling me not to do this for days, and as I stood down there waiting for the ceremony to start, he told me once again not to do this. This was not what God wanted for me. This was not who I was supposed to marry. The fear of being homeless in my head was louder than the Holy Spirit, and I walked down the aisle and pledged my heart and life to Nathan before God and everyone. We were both babies, and I don't think we truly loved each other in the way a husband and wife should. I married him out of fear of being homeless, and he married me to keep me from being homeless, but we both gave it a valiant effort at first. I sacrificed completing my last semester to achieve my college degree in order to go to work and help make us money, and he sacrificed his high school diploma for a GED so he could start training to be a welder the following year.

I ended up landing a job as a regional manager for a gym with different locations and eventually started boxing at the gym. When you fought your whole life, fighting in a closed ring with gloves and rules was a cake walk, and I was

Refined Silver

good. Really good. It didn't take much for word to get out, and I signed with a trainer to be his female boxing champion. Next thing I know, I'm popular and sought after and making 6 figures a year. Nathan never came to a single match, and I could feel us drifting apart even further every day. Within just a few months of turning 18, I got a phone call that my brother needed me to come and get him because Uncle Mark had moved him back in with Goliath months before, and Goliath had pulled a gun on him, forcing him to take off through a field and hide in the woods. I got custody of my brother and moved him in with us. I was a teenager raising a teenager. It came with complications since we were so close in age, but it was so great to be with my baby brother again. It had been years and I had missed him so much!

For 2 years, my time, energy, and talents went into boxing and raising my brother, leaving very little for my marriage. At first it was to provide money for us since he didn't work; then it was to pay for his technical college classes and apprenticeship to become a welder. I was his ATM and not much more.

One of the very few nights of intimacy gave me my precious baby boy, my very first true love. I immediately quit boxing and Nathan finally became a welder so I could stay home with my son once he was born. I grew up instantly, and my son was my entire world. I never knew you could love someone so immensely even though you hadn't met. I knew I would move mountains for my son even before he was ever born. My son gave me my greatest purpose in this life: being a mom! I had secured a vast nest egg for us from years of boxing, and Nathan was making decent money. My baby brother lived with me. Life was great, until shortly after my son's 1st birthday and I found out Nathan had stepped outside of our marriage... with several women, while I was working. I immediately move out with the knowledge that our marriage is forever over . Here is another person that was supposed to love me and respect me, and he deserted me. All of the shadows of trauma came rushing back, and if not for my son, I don't know what bad decisions I would have made. I needed him far greater than his little toddler self needed me. He saved me in ways I didn't fully realize at the time. He gave me unconditional love and purpose in a time of pain.

I never wanted my children to grow up in a broken home. So, after a couple of months of Nathan professing repentance and sorrow, promises of the world and fidelity, I moved back in. It wasn't the same. The love was lost and it was my son, my baby brother and I on one end of the trailer and Nathan on the other. On the rare occasions when he would come home. At the 4th of July celebration that year, we met up with friends and had a few drinks, and 9 months later, my oldest baby girl was born. Her perfect dimples and sapphire blue eyes instantly grew my heart a million sizes.

Refined Silver

Just when I thought I couldn't possibly love anything more, God sent me her and proved my capacity for loving someone else was an endless well. She is my perfect Christmas baby. She was due on Christmas, so I was induced on the 22nd so we would be released on Christmas Eve and get to spend Christmas all together. Imagine my surprise when it was time to leave the hospital on Christmas Eve night with our new addition and Nathan wasn't there. He was hours late, and I knew in my heart what that meant, but I pushed it down and pretended it was just my hormones.

For the next 11 months, it was my two gifts from God, my supportive baby brother, and myself most of the time. I don't know how I would have done it without my brother. He helped me with diapers and chasing a toddler, carrying the infant carrier or helping with late-night feedings. He was my confidante, my helpmate, and my best friend, but the time came for him to move on. Just 3 years after 9/11, he wanted to do his part and be in the military. Selfishly, I didn't want him to go, and I definitely didn't want to think of my baby brother overseas fighting in a war. After many talks with the recruiter and even more prayers, I gave my consent. He was 17, which required my consent. It's hard to sign your name for someone else when you know your permission could put them in danger, or worse, death. He needed structure and a strong moral man to lead him in this phase of life, and that was something I could never give him as his sister or guardian . I signed on the line, said a prayer, and gave him the longest hug before he boarded a bus bound for boot camp in another state.

Even with two little ones, the trailer seemed quieter and emptier from that point on. Especially as Nathan was gone more and more, always with an excuse of very late nights, such as the excuse of working overtime, stopping at a friend's house, etc. I was so happy being home with my children that I just readily accepted his full of holes stories until one day there was a knock at the door. With my daughter on my hip, I answered the door to find a petite woman standing on my porch. She innocently asks if Nathan is there, as I can feel the cold winter breeze rolling in. The dreary weather suddenly seems to match what I'm feeling as I tell her he is at work and inquire as to who she is.

She had the audacity to perk up and bounce up and down as she grins from ear to ear and informs me she is his girlfriend. The sky turns dark and the breeze is now a gusty wind when she asks who I am. She wasn't ready when I told her I was his wife and the mother of our 2 young children, evidenced by the way the grin on her face suddenly disappeared. I thank her for stopping by, inform her that she can find him at his parents' later that night and he would be single the by the next day , and I shut the door. I packed all of his things by nightfall and sent him to his parents.

Refined Silver

We had been sharing custody and hadn't officially separated even though we were living apart. We were in marriage counseling, and I thought we were trying to salvage the unsalvageable. Life was even harder as a single stay-at-home mom, and the fire was about to be turned up. After a couple of months of therapy and separation, there appears to be hope, so I think nothing of going down to Georgia for the weekend to help my sister move her belongings back to North Carolina. Of course, the day before my departure, my car needs repairs and has to be put into the shop. I got my first experience on a greyhound bus that converted an 8-hour ride to 19 hours. I step off the bus, and before I can even leave the bus station, I receive a text from Nathan. Attached is a video of all my belongings and most of my children's baby pictures on fire in the front yard, along with the text message informing me he had filed for divorce and had asked his girlfriend to marry him. Plot twist, she wasn't even the woman who came to my house. I immediately go to the ATM at the corner of the bus station and there is nothing in the account . All the money I had earned boxing and working, paired with what he made as a welder, had all been withdrawn. I am now in a brand new state with a small suitcase, a single mother of two children aged 2 and under, and only $5 in my pocket. A marriage I entered into to avoid being homeless, a marriage of four years, seven years together total, all up in flames literally... and now I am now homeless... in a state hours away from where I lived.

Refined Silver

I have found the one whom my soul loves-

Song of Solomon 3:4

~ 15 ~

Every year I go through our shoes to toss out the ones we no longer wear, and every year I pull out battered, ugly leather sketchers from circa 2004. Every year, I imagine what the shoes would say if they could talk. Most would see these as a worn, ugly pair of shoes, but I see survival, hard work, character, and God's plan for restoration. You see, these shoes aren't your normal pair of shoes... they have a crack on the bottom through the entire sole, so deep you can feel a draft from supporting 80-hour weeks for a very long time. They have withheld tears falling on them like London rain. They have supported a woman on a mission who never stopped. These shoes are mine. The shoes I wore on my feet when my world turned upside down and everything I had was gone. These shoes encased the feet of a girl who was suddenly transformed into a woman in the blink of an eye.

I was a young 21-year-old who stepped off a Greyhound bus with just the shoes on my feet, 2 changes of clothes, a toothbrush, a small makeup bag, and $5 to my name. Just 19 hours before, I had walked onto the bus as a wife with tens of thousands in the bank from a profitable boxing career. I was a mother of 2 young angels and had a

Refined Silver

weekend plan to help someone move. The girl before and the woman after were two vastly different people because the moment I stepped off the bus, the man I was married to was engaged to someone else. I don't know if he had planned or if he was just waiting for an opportunity, regardless he wasted no time in taking advantage of me being in another state.

He had filed for divorce, had my babies, and depleted our bank account. I was homeless, broke and all alone in the great state of Georgia, a place that I had never even visited before. I went from 2 lane highways in the Appalachian Mountains to the Mario Andretti Interstate 75. Where people either drive 90 mph, and weave in or out of traffic. Or were like pace cars, going 20 mph and holding all the cars back. If you have ever driven in Atlanta, you know exactly what I'm talking about. These shoes sat in front of the couch of a friend of a friend that I crashed on. These shoes walked me to a bar and grill the next day, not for a drink but for a job, and then a second job and a third. These shoes had Kentucky dirt in the soles but Georgia sweat and determination in the owner; determination to make a life worth living for herself, but most of all her children. These shoes have seen me through it all; through getting a car, an apartment, money in the bank, clothes in my closet and everything my children could desire. These shoes saw me through a divorce, hitting rock bottom as well as leaping hurdles and falling into the arms of my prince charming.

They saw me through a costly, exhausting custody battle; through the hardest trials I've faced in my life; and some of the happiest memories a woman could ever have.

Every year I struggle to throw away these worn, ugly, and out-of-date shoes, so every year I slide them back into the corner of my closet; a silent reminder of who I am, where I've been, the journey God brought me through, and the strength I hold inside. They're a promise to myself that no matter what, this brown-eyed girl in her brown shoes can overcome anything with God on her side; that it's not the shoes on the feet that make the person... it's the grit and character they have inside of them and God's grace upon them...

I couldn't move in with my sister since she was moving into a HUD apartment in North Carolina and I had nowhere to stay if I went back to Kentucky. Thankfully, a friend of a friend in Kennesaw, Georgia, had offered their couch for me to sleep on until I got on my feet.

If I was going to start all over, what better place than somewhere where I could truly have a fresh start? Even if I wanted to go back, I didn't have enough money to get to the grocery store, let alone back to Kentucky. The next day, I walked up and down Wade Green Road, putting in applications to any place I could get hired. Thankfully, a bar and grill owner took sympathy for my current circumstances and hired me on the spot as the only dayshift waitress. It allowed me to make money immediately and was only 2 miles from where I was staying, so I could walk back and forth to work. I worked 6 days a week and saved up every penny I could. By the end of the month, I had a second job as an assistant teacher at a pre-k/daycare. This allowed me to get free childcare while I got back on my feet and ensured my children were with me as much as possible. By the end of the year, I was divorced, working 3 jobs, and preparing for the most contentious custody battle.

Nathan didn't want the kids. He rarely spent time with them since they were born and he was living his best life with his new fiancée. Two little children get in the way of drinking and partying. Regardless, the need to inflict as much pain on me as possible was greater, and he knew my kids were the way to get to me. Since I had been a ward of the state before we were married, everything was in his name, including my car, which he promptly sold to buy his fiancée an engagement ring. It angered him that I didn't care about any of it. I just wanted my children and a clean break, which meant, of course, my children were pawns in this game he created, a game that drugged out for years. Two years later, I had worked my way up from nothing and now had a vehicle, an apartment, and a replacement of all that was charred to ashes a couple of years before. I'm still in a contentiously long, arduous custody battle. Nathan's family were well known, had money, a good family name, and were friends with the Judge. I had to hire an expensive attorney, one that cost me around $3,000 due to filing, attorney fees, court fees, hotel, and gas for every hearing. We had at least one hearing every 3 months.

During this time, I was a deputy sheriff jailer, a bouncer at a nightclub, a cashier at Dunkin' Donuts, and a cosmetologist's assistant. Monday through Thursday, my day usually consisted of getting up at 5 am to be at Dunkin by 6 am to open the store. I would work from 6 to 10 am and then go a couple of stores down to the hair salon. I worked as an assistant there from 10:30 until 2 pm, went back to my apartment to shower, and be at the jail by 4 pm, then worked until midnight. I would go home exhausted and crash the moment I walked in the door, only to get up the next morning at 5 am to start again. On the weekends, I would work at the jail during the day, come home and nap for a couple of hours until it was time to go to the club/bar for my bouncer job until the club closed for the night, usually 2 or 3 in the morning.

The cost of rent and food in Kennesaw were high, and I needed every penny I could earn, so I ended up sharing an apartment with the most flamboyant roommate you could ever imagine, trying to save as much money as possible. Close your eyes. Now imagine the Buffalo Bill character from *Silence of the Lambs* twirling in his robe. Now take out the whole sadistic "it puts the lotion on its skin." Got the

Refined Silver

image? Now, add in Mark Hoppus from Blink 182 but shrink him down to 5 feet and you have pictured my roommate. I'd been divorced for years but was still bitter and over men by this point. I had tried dating a few times, and it always ended in disaster, slowly transforming me into an "I am woman, hear me roar" broken and angry woman. I was loud, brash, and took no prisoners, and men were the least of my concerns. Then, God sent me a stripper, and that changed everything. OK, not really a stripper, but that's where this part of the story really starts.

Myspace was all the rage, if any of the younger generation are reading this….it was the original Facebook, but cooler. The most drama you ever had was choosing your Top 8 friends or being removed from the Top 8. Eeekkk! My roommate was technologically handicapped but wanted to try online social media. I sat there on our couch on a Tuesday evening, logged into my account, helping my inept friend while completely unaware my life was going to change in just a few keystrokes. Myspace had a search option where you could input parameters in your search and it would pull people that met those parameters, such as a 50-mile radius, male or female, etc. I was showing him how to search and send messages when this dark-haired, fit, arms crossed as he leaned against his white mustang, with the world is my playground sly grin on his face…. gorgeous dream pops up.

Refined Silver

I sent him a request and message, expecting nothing more than the typical cheesy one-liners guys usually send. His profile said he was a stripper and was filled with pictures of his car and motorcycle, none of which would normally get a second glance from me. We started messaging, and it was like an "Invasion of Body Snatchers" was playing out in my living room as I broke a cardinal rule and gave him my phone number. He called me instantly, and for the next 8 hours straight, we talked about anything and everything. He proudly told me he was a State Trooper which I thought he meant he dressed as a character he played when he was dancing. I went on a tirade of how insulting it is to the men and women who risk their lives every day, as he just chuckled and lets me finish before he corrected me. He was never a stripper although he had the body of one. He had lost a dare and had to put stripper as his occupation as the losing consequence. He really was a State Trooper that worked and lived one county over. One who wasn't interested in women with tattoos or a loud mouth, and I wasn't interested in dating someone in a uniform. I had never been a badge bunny and had no interest in being one now.

Both of us had all the qualities that the other one didn't want in a partner, and yet we just kept talking all night. There was a supernatural comfort, as though I had known him my entire life. We spoke of childhood memories as though we both experienced them together. The moment he said hello, my brain rewired and I couldn't remember a single moment before him. The sensible and cautious woman I was/am went out the window. I swear something had taken over my body because not only did I tell him my deepest, darkest secrets, but when he asked me out on a date the following day and I declined him because it was American Idol night...I invited him to my apartment for an American Idol date night. I never gave strangers my number, ever! I never brought a man to my apartment ever! I was guarded with people, I didn't tell them my secrets or desires. I didn't trust people, especially men. Yet, here I was completely breaking all the rules without a hint of trepidation.

He showed up with $60 of Chinese food because he remembered Chinese is my favorite. He sat on my couch and watched American Idol without complaint. As if that wasn't an indication he was a Saint, the fact he sat there for hours and listened to my eccentric liberal roommate's views on politics, music, weather, etc. and never said a cross word. It spoke volumes of his patience, and Lord knows, people need A LOT of patience when dealing with me. By the time he left that night, I knew he was my forever and I, his. It was as though I had spent my entire life thinking my soul was whole, and then he walked into my life and I felt my soul was complete for the first time. Two days later, he took me home to meet his parents, and on the fifth day, we moved in together. (I have told my children if they ever even thought about doing something like that, I would tie them up in their rooms until they are 45.)

A month later, we were at his parents' visiting, and I got a phone call that the custody battle had just heated up and was going to cost even more. I was tapped out—financially, mentally, and emotionally. I had hit my breaking point. The invisible dam inside of me broke, and I just started uncontrollably bawling. To get some fresh air, he suggested we go for a midnight walk under the stars. His parents lived on a stretch of paved road that is just straight land for miles. You could see a car in the distance and still have 4 minutes to get out of the road before it reaches you. We walked up and down the road for an hour before sitting down in the middle of the quiet road. There is something magical when you're able to sit on a double yellow line without danger, surrounded by nothing but nature, singing all around you as the night sky puts on a show.

It was spring, but the night air still had a slight crispness to it. The stars filled the sky, twinkling as though they were performing their greatest symphony as the insects and frogs played accompanying music. The moon was so full and bright that it cascades our shadows onto the pavement. I'm sitting there devastated as a mother when I look at our shadows of him holding me in his arms, and it's not only pain I'm feeling now, but joy too. It's such an overwhelming experience because I am in this doubled-over, hard to breathe, beyond devastation, heartache over my children, yet Tom Cruise's jump on the couch, joy at seeing myself in his arms. I tell him that I'm going to have to pause the custody fight because I have hit rock bottom. I don't have the financial means to sustain another hearing, let alone years. When he loudly exclaims, "That is never going to happen. That we will both work a million jobs or sell everything we own if need be. Whatever it takes," he will not let me quit until they are home with us forever.

Up until that point, I didn't even know he had any other tone of voice besides his calming one. It was the sweetest (and honestly sexiest) thing I have ever seen in a man to see him go from loving support to a fierce protector and leader so quickly. All the men in my life had always been loud and angry or meek and wise. I had never seen a bold yet loving man take charge before then. At that very moment, I knew I wanted him to be the one to forever lead our family. I asked him to marry me and he said yes. Actually, he said, he was already planning on asking me the following week, and had it all planned out but I beat him to it and ruined the surprise, but yes….he was down for whatever. Let the record show, I asked first. I love him more.

We got married at the courthouse 5 months later in jeans and his mismatched shoes, which he accidentally wore due to nerves. For the first 45 minutes of being Mrs. Lawrence, he was on the phone with a female… the D.A. for an upcoming vehicular homicide trial in which he had to testify. It should have been an indication of our future as that pretty much sums up being married to a first responder. I had stopped believing in fairy tales long before, but he taught me to believe in them again. He was my knight in shining armor (or Kevlar), he loved me for me, physical and emotional scars and all. I've never been so overjoyed to make a promise to someone as I was when I said my vows and took his last name. I have read enough fairy tales to know what comes after getting married to your Prince Charming.

And they lived happily ever after…

Refined Silver

But he said to me, "My grace is sufficient for you, for my power is made perfect in weakness." Therefore I will boast all the more gladly of my weaknesses, so that the power of Christ may rest upon me.

2nd Corinthians 12:9

~ 16 ~

Disney princess movies always end with "Happily Ever After" but never show you what the "after" looks like. You know why? Because it's messy. It's joy and laughter, tears and heartache, arguments and makeup, between overworked and underpaid, sickness and health...messy life. In the mess is where the real magic happens though; where marriages are strengthened, friendships forged, where our faith is nurtured, intimacy with Christ is cultivated, and where God does the most work on us.

Within the first couple years of marriage, we experienced a lot of mess, such as going from a two-person income to one. I had left the S.O. and my other jobs to move down to his parents' in south Georgia. We were relocating there as soon as my husband got a transfer, and I wanted to get a jump start before we settled. Once I had moved, I couldn't find work. It was during the time of previous White House administration and jobs were hard to find. Since I was a transplant, it was even harder for me because people down there have known each other for generations. An outsider was like a scarlet letter, or worse, a Yankee.*gasp* I was not getting any of the few jobs available. Those were reserved for people they knew their entire lives.

Refined Silver

We experienced losing family members, demotions, relocations, house fires, and floods; and a lot of people were upset that my husband married a single mother, especially one that he hadn't known for long. As well as the on your-knees painful messiness of life, such as having a miscarriage and then being told you can never have children again. We experienced really meager living, especially when most of the money went to attorneys and trips back and forth to court. Our first apartment furniture consisted of a mattress on the floor and a 20-year-old TV on a black spray-painted dollar general cardboard box. We had four plastic plates and cups, one pan, and three towels. Food for my husband and I was meager as well. Thankfully, Chick-fil-A kept us from starving since they always gave law enforcement their meals for free. Even though my husband is mildly allergic to peanuts, he would eat there every day so that we could both eat. He would order a meal with an additional sandwich to bring home for me to eat at the end of his shift. While the kids ate Spaghetti O's, hotdogs and Mac and cheese, or hotdogs and syrup, he and I usually ate once a day, usually an old chicken sandwich. We created "struggle meals" that to this day are some of my family's favorites, such as 2 slices of BBQ pork tenderloin cut up into bite-size pieces and mixed in with 2 packs of beef Ramen for a dinner of four. For special treats, we would have a flour tortilla that was pan fried and coated with cinnamon sugar, topped with 1 tablespoon of peanut butter and 2 marshmallows. Put it under the broiler until the marshmallows melt, then drizzle with chocolate syrup and enjoy the delectable and gooey treat.

When life is hard, "wins" are that much sweeter. We finally won full custody, which was also the last day we ever saw or heard from Nathan. Once he lost, his game was over, and he wanted nothing to do with the children. My husband forever adopted them as his children without even a second thought or hesitation. They weren't the only ones that were forever claimed. The Millers and I found each other again and, as they say, the rest is history. I finally had parents who wanted me, a family that loved me and called me their daughter. Being able to call my mom or dad for advice or share jokes with my siblings was something I never thought I would have, but God blessed me tenfold with my family!

Our children longed for another sibling, one that I knew we weren't able to give them. They wanted a little brother or sister so badly that our oldest daughter wished for a baby sister that Christmas. We chuckled and told her Santa doesn't bring those kinds of gifts. Well... 9 months later, the healthy and beautiful baby girl that had us all wrapped around her newborn pinkie would say otherwise. The doctors that told us we couldn't have any more children may know science and medical care, but they didn't know my God. He gave us the answer to our prayers and our daughter's Christmas wish. Every year since, we have a running joke that our oldest daughter wishes for ridiculously lavish things like an 8,000 sq. ft. house or a million dollars. My family was all together, my husband was thriving at work, finances were better, our family was perfect… we had the all American life.

In the fall of 2011, I stopped having menstrual cycles all together, and I was exhausted all the time, regardless of whether I had slept 15 hours. Our sex life took a hit as it was so painful it would take my breath away… not in a good way either. I had chalked it up to hormones trying to settle since it had been about a year since our little rainbow baby was born. When March of the following year rolls around, I'm hit with the familiar nausea that only comes with morning sickness. I didn't know how it was possible, but I knew I was pregnant again. I went to the doctor to confirm the pregnancy, and sure enough, we were expecting. During my examination, my doctor's facial expression went from normal to concerned quite rapidly. He tells me I have a moderate sized spot on my cervix and he needs to do a biopsy. I wasn't exactly sure what that meant, but I didn't think it was in the risk factors or anything significant. I didn't have multiple sex partners, I was in my 20s, and I had never had an abnormal Pap smear. I don't know if I was just blissfully ignorant or consumed with joy that we were having another baby, but I wasn't concerned about it at all.

Refined Silver

The next day, I'm in the kitchen starting dinner. My husband is at work and the kids are in the living room playing with their toys and watching Shrek. When my phone rings, it sounds different than it ever has before, as though suddenly time has slowed down and faded as the phone rings slowly. Without even looking at the caller ID, I immediately know it's my doctor and something is wrong, as if my heart and soul knew before my brain did. I answer to hear my doctor on the other end. My internal alarms in my head are now going off. My doctor has never personally called me. If something is needed, a nurse or someone from his office calls and relays the results. If he is calling, this must not be good news. He makes idle pleasantries as my nerves are shaking, waiting to hear why he really called. He tells me my biopsy came back... Stage 1 cervical cancer.

I don't know what he has said after that, as I stand there frozen in time in a haze. The moment I heard cancer, the world stopped. Somehow, we get off the phone, I very well may have hung up on him. I don't know, my mind went blank. I'm standing there watching my 3 children, all under the age of 8, dance and play without a care in the world. The realization hits me that 5 minutes ago life was perfect and now it may not ever be again. It hits me like a semi-truck barreling out of control before slamming into a wall. I step outside on the back porch, out of the children's sight, so they don't see me, and I break down. I am in my 20s. I have young children who need me! Heck, I have a tiny baby inside of me that literally needs me in order to survive. How is this possible? What does it mean? I didn't even ask the doctor any questions. I have no idea what to do next. After a couple of minutes of questions running through my mind, I call my husband and tell him that he needs to come home.

The moment he arrives, something changes. I'm no longer concerned for me, I'm concerned for him. This is going to devastate him. How do I tell him, especially without any answers to the millions of questions he is naturally going to have? He is standing there, looking so tall and fine in his crisp blue uniform, but the moment I tell him the news, he crumbles and starts crying as though I have shattered his heart. I hate the pain that I just caused him. It breaks my heart to see the tears rolling down his face as he wraps his arms around me, fully engulfing me. Apparently, he needs me more than I need oxygen because he is holding me so tightly I can't breathe. I console him and tell him it will be OK, somehow, someway, it will be OK. After some time, his radio breaks up our embrace. There is a serious wreck on the ground, and they need him more than I do at the moment. We agree not to tell anyone until we know more and no matter what, we don't want the kids to know and worry. A kiss goodbye and he's off to save the world with the weight of the world on his shoulders.

The next day, my husband and I sit across from my doctor as he explains that this is unknown territory. Most women with cervical cancer can't get pregnant, so there aren't many cases of women having cervical cancer while pregnant. There is also a strong possibility the cancer could spread rapidly because of my hormones while pregnant. Cervical cancer is normally a slow-progressing cancer that takes years to form and progress. Yet, the postpartum hormones from having a child the year before has progressed the cancer from nothing to Stage 1 within a year, so what will happen during these 9 months? After discussing the risks, he asks if we want to have an abortion, without even discussing it with each other. My husband and I both say "No" in unison. For the sake of our unborn child's safety, we forego any additional diagnostic tests and any cancer treatment until she is born. The doctor tells us I will need a total hysterectomy pretty much as soon as she is born, and if the cancer has spread outside of the cervix or uterus, I will have to do chemo and radiation. The cancer is mere inches from my unborn child. Will it affect her any? Will my cervix fail to stay closed and protect my child from infection or premature birth? There are a lot of unknown variables that we can't even come up with a plan for because we don't even know what they are. We just know that I am going to fight like hell to grow and deliver this beautiful child and then fight like hell to beat cancer, whatever the cost.

Each week that my pregnancy progresses, I lose more weight and hair from the cancer. To make matters worse, I also have severe morning sickness. Why do they call it morning sickness? Mine lasts morning, noon, and night during the entire pregnancy and when there is nothing to throw up, does that stop? Nope, I dry heave. I digress. At our 16-week ultrasound, we find out we are having a beautiful baby girl, but they are concerned about her lack of growth and the length of her nose. They suspect she may have Down's Syndrome and want to do an amniocentesis to verify. We agree to the test but are very clear, regardless of what the test shows, "we are keeping her, so don't even ask!" She ends up not having Down's Syndrome, but my body is struggling to support her growth. She is tiny and struggling, so I'm put on supplement drinks and medicine 3 times a day. I'm still getting weaker every day. I've lost so much weight that my skin is literally hanging from my bones. My body can't produce very much amniotic fluid. How much longer can she hold on? The reality that I may die is becoming more present every day. I'm not afraid of dying for me, I am afraid for my family. Am I going to leave my small children motherless? Will my young husband become a widower with 3 small children? If I make it through the pregnancy, will my baby girl always have growth problems or physical issues that we don't know about yet? Will the cancer affect her genetic makeup? Lord, my life is finally perfect… Please don't let me die. Don't let my unborn child die! We already lost one child in a miscarriage, I can't bare to lose another.

Refined Silver

The fear of the unknown future is almost paralyzing and dominates my thoughts when I'm awake and my dreams when I sleep. I was so worried about what might happen that it was robbing me of my present. I spent so much of my time begging God to save my daughter and me instead of just trusting God to be with us every step of the way. We finally decide to give it all to God and let it go. Whatever happens is his will. Who was I to question it? None of this was in our control, and the weight of it is almost crippling. God has given us another miracle wrapped up in a miracle. Why would he take it away? He is a loving Father, not a cruel one. He doesn't give just to snatch it away and cause devastation. My God is faithful; he has never failed me and I know he will not fail me now. My baby girl saved my life. Without her, I am scared to think what would have happened. My husband and I were always faithful to one another, and I was young, so I didn't get annual Pap smears. I didn't think I needed to. I wasn't at risk of anything, or so I thought.

Even though it should have been obvious that something was amiss, I had excused away all the warning signs of cancer. Had I not been pregnant, it would have been years of the cancer spreading throughout my body before I would have gone to the doctor. Chances are, it would have been too late and too advanced by the time it would have been discovered. God saved me by sending us our baby girl, and I knew he would sustain us through this. My husband

Refined Silver

and I stopped worrying and started fully trusting God. At 35 weeks pregnant, I weigh 35 lbs less than I did when I found out I was pregnant, but our little bundle of joy is born. She is healthy and perfect, we even get to leave the hospital after 3 days....and less than 5 lbs.

We have 4 weeks to get my body as healthy as possible for my surgery. Thankfully, it seemed to be contained to my uterus and cervix, but they wouldn't know for sure until I was on the operating table. I was so afraid my body couldn't handle the surgery and recovery. I had very little meat on my bones to the point where my veins actually protruded. I was so anemic that if you looked at me for too long, I would bruise. As I held my baby girl and looked at our perfectly complete family of 6, I was worried I wouldn't make it off the table or that I would end up needing chemo, and I knew my body couldn't handle chemo as sick as I already was.

I've always been a planner, someone who plans for all scenarios, someone who is prepared regardless of what comes their way. It's how I ensure my survival regardless of the situation. Unfortunately, with cancer, it's hard to be prepared because everything is unknown. So I prepared the best I could. I sat down and wrote a letter to my husband and each of our children about how much I loved them and how they were blessings from God and the good in my life. I then wrote them all letters for special occasions such as birthdays 1-18, proms, graduations, first breakups, weddings, and births of their children. I then wrote letters to my husband for our future anniversaries and gave him how-to advice to get him through all the same special occasions I wrote to the children about. I wrote letters to my parents and in-laws thanking them for all they did, and then I wrote letters of forgiveness to every family member, foster care family, and abuser. I wrote so much that I am pretty sure I cleared an entire land mass of trees to supply the paper.

I always put up my Christmas on the night of Thanksgiving, when the whole family is home and in good cheer. Unfortunately, my surgery was scheduled for the day before Thanksgiving. I was worried I would be sick if I had to do chemo and my family wouldn't have a Christmas tree. I was worried my surgery and recovery would prevent them from having a magical Christmas. But most of all, I feared the worst: and that my family would lose me and not have Christmas at all. That was unacceptable, because Christmas is the most magical time of the year; a time of hope, wishing, and joy; when humanity is at its best and, above all… God's saving grace. I knew that if my family lost me, they wouldn't put up a tree, they wouldn't place jingle bells and twinkling lights throughout the house. They wouldn't care for Christmas ever again. As a headstrong, stubborn warrior, I wasn't about to let cancer have that power over Christmas. I may not have been able to control what it was doing to my body, but by God I could make sure Christmas was magical and ready to go even if I wasn't there. I put up the Christmas tree on November 1st, and it changed my entire magical holiday season from then on. Every year since, I have continued the November 1st tree lighting, partly as a reminder and celebration that God brought our family through such a hard time, but also because I learned a valuable lesson that year. I learned many lessons actually, especially never taking for granted the day, hour, or second you have in this world. I realized that I wasn't as stressed throughout the season, that my spirit was lighter and I had more time with my family throughout the season. That first year, I thought maybe it was because I had just been served a huge wake-up call, but I noticed the same thing the following year, and the year after.

Christmas lights have always stirred this comfort in me, like my grandma's piping hot chocolatey cup of hot cocoa with extra marshmallows on a cold and snowy day, where one sip warms your body and soul. I mean, have you ever sat beside a Christmas tree at night with all the lights off except the tree and watched how the lights bounce off the glittery globes and homemade ornaments? It's mesmerizing, and who has ever looked at Christmas lights and felt anger or sadness? No one, not even the Grinch! Every had a bad day, then walk into your mom's house during the holidays and the scent of cinnamon and baking holiday sweets hit you; Santa and angel figurines singing and Christmas carols playing in the background. Suddenly, your bad day melts away... why not have more of those days? We have all become so busy with bake sales, Christmas programs, shopping and wrapping, trying to finish decorating and the million things we try to cram in during 30 days of madness. We are surrounded by negativity from the media, deadlines, and drama at work, chaos at home or in the community. Our lives are filled with constant pressure from all angles, and it weighs on you. Everyone could use a little more magic in their lives; the comfort of home, the joy of your inner child excited for Santa and, most of all, hope. I mean, isn't that what Christmas is about—God faithfully sending us hope? God loving us so much that he sent a little baby to save us all, to give us hope and faith, joy and love.

So, I challenge you to stop trying to shove it all into a four-week window, put your tree up early, turn on some Christmas carols and grab that magic as soon as you can! Life is always going to be messy, but "Happily Ever After" is found in Christ and his saving love. It's found in God's sustaining grace and the Holy Spirit's calming peace. It's found in your husband, broken-hearted over something happening to you, or when he holds your hair back every day as you throw up. It's found in the way he holds your hand as you're wheeled off to surgery. It's the innocence of children laughing or the way a newborn wraps their hand around your finger. It's found in Christmas lights bouncing off of glittery ornaments. It's found mixed up in the mess of life. You just have to know where to look.

Refined Silver

"Behold, blessed is the one whom God reproves; therefore despise not the discipline of the Almighty. For he wounds, but he binds up; he shatters, but his hands heal.
Job 5:17-18

~ 17 ~

In the fall of 2015, my entire family and I contracted Rotavirus. Let me tell you, seven years later, I still feel queasy thinking about it. Moms never get sick days, especially when the whole family is sick. It was so bad, I had to have a puke bucket with me when I cleaned up everyone else's vomit. Three bathrooms in our house quickly felt like zero bathrooms. I have never been that sick in my life! Right after getting over that virus, the whole family contracted Flu B. Two weeks later, we got hit with another wave of sickness, one that made it hard to even keep our eyes open while walking. I kid you not, I went to take a popsicle upstairs to one of the children and had to stop and sit on the stairs before even making it to the landing, where I promptly fell asleep, only to wake up hours later covered in melted popsicle. We went back to the doctor, who told us it was just our bodies' trying to cope with all the illnesses.

Unbeknownst to us, we had came down with the Epstein-Barr Virus (EBV), also known as the strain that causes mono. We had contracted EBV right on the heels of Rotavirus and Flu B. Our immune systems had been seriously compromised by the previous viruses. As a result, EBV was able to infiltrate our T cells, awakening unknown dormant genetically inherited autoimmune and auto-inflammatory diseases. Since we didn't know at the time that we had EBV, our oldest two children and the littlest one had received immunizations or boosters during that time period. It was like pouring gasoline on a rapidly growing wildfire.

By March, our oldest (son) suddenly had a large mass appear on his leg beneath his knee. Within a month his limbs would turn red like a lobster and swell, shortly after that he began having moderate swelling in his chest and arm pits. He began having debilitating body pains that was so severe, the pain had him on the floor in a fetal position. He never had headaches before but suddenly he was getting them everyday. The doctors first thought it was Osgood-Schlatter disease, a common issue among runners. I knew that couldn't possibly be my son's case, he was more of a gamer than an active sports kind of kid. They told me they were certain it was Osgood and I was overly concerned, but I refused to accept it without even doing an x-ray or blood work.

Once they ran blood work, it became clear this was more serious. His white blood cells were alarmingly high, in the 30,000 to 50,000 range. The normal range for an 11-year-old is around 8,000 white blood cells. His liver was not working properly, and no one could tell us why. All his doctor could do was send us to a specialist, but he was unsure of who to actually send us to. He wasn't even sure what the problem was. So they first sent us to an allergy specialist but he wasn't allergic to anything. Then they sent us the Children's Hospital, where we were sent to endocrinologist(doctors who treat endocrine issues such as hormones disorders like thyroid issues.) When they couldn't find anything, they sent us to an orthopedic(a bone doctor). Either they couldn't find anything or they found more issues such as lytic lesions(whole in his spine) but not the cause. So they sent us to another "ologist", until we had practically seen every type of "ologist" the Children's Hospital had. He has become a human pin cushion. In 2 years, he had over 300 vials of blood drawn for tests, over 30 x-rays and 3 MRI.

For a family that had never been sick, outside of having cancer or the occasional case of strep throat or flu, it was scary and overwhelming. Our oldest daughter was diagnosed with Tourette's when she was six, but it had never caused actual health issues. We were in uncharted territory now. I had never seen anything like this; everyone was healthy, and then we just woke up one day, and everything had changed in an instant. It seemed like we couldn't stop getting sick.

In the process of trying to figure out what is happening to our oldest child, our oldest daughter's health starts declining. She gained 40 lbs. in a matter of 2 months, even though she was incredibly active and rarely ate junk food, meat, or fast food. She would turn ghost white suddenly as though she had been drained of all the blood in her body and lose all feeling in her hands without any cause or explanation. She was constantly freezing, the kind where she would sleep under two comforters and still be cold in our 74° house. She would lie on the floor crying because her stomach and joints were hurting so badly. Tylenol and Motrin did nothing for the pain and it was only getting more severe. To make matters worse, her kidneys stopped filtering properly, so she began to have blood in her urine. Like with our oldest, the doctors couldn't tell us what was happening, only that she was sick, which we obviously knew. We began cycling through specialists. They would send us to a nephrologist(a kidney doctor), who would tell us her kidneys were struggling they didn't know why. So they sent us to an endocrinologist(doctor for hormones syndromes such hypo-thyroidism) who would run test after test and then send us to another "ologist."

Our youngest(daughter) has had occasional bouts of fever accompanied by face swelling and joint pain ever since she was 2 weeks old. It would only happen occasionally, and no more than once or twice a year. The doctors would always check her out and play it off as seasonal allergies. Beginning in 2016, it started happening every 4 weeks like clockwork. Every month, the flare-ups would last longer, and her fevers would get higher. She would complain of severe stomach and joint pain all the week prior, and by the next week she would have a continuous fever that would rise as high as 106° or 107° F. To the point, she would be as red as a lobster and almost too hot to touch. Imagine the worst sunburn you ever had, how blistering deep red your skin was, and how the heat would radiate from your skin and through your clothes. It was like that the entire week of a flare-up.

She would be so weak from the combination of high fevers and inability to eat anything other than popsicles. that her legs would shake uncontrollably when she stood, as though she were seizing. A few times she actually did have febrile seizures that would send us to the hospital for the night. She would lie helpless in bed for a week at a time. The usual remedies such as Tylenol, Ibuprofen, and tepid baths did nothing. As quickly as it came on, it would suddenly come down and pass. This happened every month, and of course, her pediatrician sent us on a specialist crusade for her as well. My perfect and healthy family now had three members down and out. No one could tell us why or how to fix it. After a year of nonstop issues, I became overwhelmed and brokenhearted; I started to lose faith, especially when the doctors sent our oldest to the Aflac Cancer Center because they feared he had leukemia.

Thankfully, after a bone marrow biopsy, they confirmed it wasn't leukemia, but they couldn't tell us what was happening, only that he was getting worse. His blood was attacking itself, and he now had a lytic lesion (a hole) in the base of his spine and three cysts in his sinuses, including one by his brain. 2016 comes and goes; there are no answers to what is happening to 3 of my 4 children, but the specialists and the surgeries keep piling up. We have an "ologist" of every kind. The more I have on my plate, the more I become upset with God for not fixing my children, and the more I pull away from him. We end the year and bring in the new one with our youngest having her tonsils and adenoids removed to help with her flare-ups. Our oldest went on hospital homebound from school to have surgery to remove the cysts. Our oldest daughter's kidneys were getting worse, and she was in too much pain and too weak to even walk down the stairs. She wakes up one night struggling to breathe and so weak she can barely stand. She is freezing, even under multiple blankets. She tries to walk to my room and wake me up, but as she gets one foot outside her door, she passes out. Mother's instinct wakes me up, and I find her passed out in front of her bedroom door. Once again, doctors can't tell us why.

Every week, I am juggling an appointment at the Children's Hospital for one of the kids, sometimes multiple appointments. I am watching the decline of my children, completely helpless as a mother because I can't fix it. I can't even get answers to what's happening. To top it all off, I have to have my own surgery on my ankle to remove the screws and metal plates that have started to work their way out, all while driving my children to and from each school every day, serving as a board member on the PTO, running our household, coaching sports and being the wife of a state trooper who worked long hours and different shifts every day.

I rang in 2017 believing that the year would be different, that it would get better... well, it got worse. We had been released from the Cancer Center for our oldest since it wasn't cancer, which was great news, but he was still declining and there were still no answers. They sent him to immunologists who were in contact with the National Institute of Health to try to get suggestions. The endocrinologist thought our oldest daughter had lupus, and our youngest had been diagnosed with a rare form of Periodic Fever Syndrome called HIDS. The type she has is one you don't outgrow; like the more common version, she will live with issues from this one for the rest of her life. Finally having answers should have been a relief, but it was another blow to the gut. Every time I looked at her angelic face, I would see her as an adult, in pain and having a flareup while trying to hold down her career and raise her family. My heart hurt thinking about her future, all because we got sick and had caught Epstein-Barr, which activated these diseases we had inherited but never knew lay dormant in our bodies. My family had been attacked, and there was nothing I could do to prevent it, nothing I could do to stop it. A single virus chewed us up and spit out the remains.

In February of 2017, we went out to eat Chinese for Valentine's Day with the family. That day, we decided to just stop thinking about everything and just enjoy the day. At this particular restaurant, there was a single entrance and exit that took you beside a water fountain, encased in a tile enclosure. Next to it was a set of gumball machines, attached to the tile with a heavy metal pipe. When we were leaving, unbeknownst to us, there was a huge puddle of water in the walkway, and our middle daughter had slipped in it as she sprinted towards the gumball machines. She hit the side of her head on the metal pole and then the tile... hard. People in the restaurant had frozen fear on their faces after hearing it so loudly. We immediately took her to the emergency room. Thankfully, she didn't fracture her skull. They tell us she has a concussion, to take her home to rest for the weekend, and to monitor her. By Monday, she was getting worse. She was having severe ear pain and headaches, and her behavior had changed. Her pediatrician determined she had post-concussion syndrome.

Within a week, she started having seizures. When she had a seizure, her vision would suddenly go black and all four of her limbs would temporarily become paralyzed, as though her brain and body would temporarily power down. When it came back online, she would be so exhausted that she would sleep for 16 hours straight. She was diagnosed with post-traumatic brain injury-induced epilepsy. One fall had changed her entire world. The area that was damaged was her left temporal lobe. The left lobe controls and processes emotions, language, and certain aspects of visual perception. The left temporal lobe is her dominant side. It involves understanding language and learning and remembering verbal information. She began to have severe anxiety and obsessive-compulsive disorder from that point on. The happy and adventurous little girl was gone, replaced with an anxiety-driven little girl. A little girl who went as far as running in front of a bus at school to try to keep me from driving off when I dropped her off at school because she was suddenly afraid of everything. On top of doctor visits, we added a therapist to the ever-growing list.

Every single one of my healthy children were no longer "healthy". They were injured and sick replicas of the children they were before. They were tired of being sick and confused; we all were. We had hit rock bottom; we were in serious debt from all the doctors' bills. I had started to become depressed as my entire world was falling apart. The kids were missing school weekly for doctor's appointments or sickness, even though it was excused. The school said they understood, but you could feel the tension, especially after I quit as a board member on the PTO. Friends I thought would be there for life were gone. They weren't really friends at all. Apparently, tough times have an expiration date. You can only be sick or broken for so long, before some people leave. I had become a shell of the person I was. I became deeply depressed, stopped eating, and smoked cigarettes like a choo-choo train. I cried myself to sleep at night and put on a fake smile in the morning. I pulled away from my husband and everyone else. My soul was tired. I was so stressed that I gave myself a bleeding ulcer and missed my son's 13th birthday because I was in the hospital, literally throwing up blood. To this day, my heart breaks that he missed such an important day because of me.

That August, the school came after us, claiming neglect caused by education deprivation. They said we neglected our straight-A students because they missed so much school the previous year. Yes, I said previous, the year that was already finished. My children were on the honor roll, in spite of all their health issues and doctor appointments. Additionally, my children had some of the highest test scores in the county and were in gifted classes. They even made the local newspaper for nationally acclaimed awards. It didn't matter that each day was excused; it didn't matter that they knew how sick the kids were and we were doing everything we could to keep from drowning. All that mattered to them was that they were losing money because it was a Title l school. Title l schools in Georgia are required to meet a quota of attendees each day for funding. We had to hire two attorneys and start homeschooling our children immediately, which was more stress and betrayal. The charges were later dropped, and they admitted in court that they actually erased excused absences just to get us into court. Their hope was to force the children to come to school even if they were sick or to un-enroll our children so as not to hurt their funding. They treated our chronically sick children as if they has the sniffles and should suck it and muster through. The reality is they did muster through, they showed up countless times and always gave their 100%.

It didn't matter what the reason was; it was inexcusable and one of the many things that wrong with public schools. They do not see our children as children, they see them as $, vessels ripe for indoctrination, squashing out all individual characteristics and replaced with robots. Recess is long gone, as are most field trips and extra curricular activities. Where our children are heavily burdened with hours of homework, unheard parents, and overworked and undervalued teachers try their best in a system that has money and government policies at the forefront, ahead of our communities. They tried to ruin our reputation and could have cost my husband his career and our health insurance… all for money.

Refined Silver

I had hit rock bottom. I was angry with God; how could he allow this to happen to my kids? He owed me for my tragic childhood filled with violence and molestation, bouncing from place to place, and never once did I lose sight of him. I had proved my love and loyalty to him my entire life.

Through every struggle and every trial, I sang his praise. How dare he let Satan mess with my kids? In the Fall of 2017, our oldest was being sent back to Aflac Cancer Center with a partially collapsed lung, an enlarged liver and spleen, and the knowledge that his problems stemmed from his bone marrow. He would need a bone marrow transplant. Our oldest daughter was not any better. We still didn't have answers, which meant no treatment. We could only watch her get worse and worse and do nothing about it. Our middle daughter was still filled with anxiety as well as seizures and had to be moved into our room at night to be monitored, as her seizures were the worst at night. Our youngest daughter's surgery had fixed her fevers, unless she got sick or had immunizations. Yet there was nothing they could do for the joint pain and swelling or the pain in her stomach from the internal swelling during a flare-up.

In November of 2017, I lost it. I called my father-in-law, a man who wasn't just my husband's dad but was like mine as well. I called him and told him my soul was tired. He told me to talk to God. I argued that I had, but he wasn't

Refined Silver

listening; he had left me! Pa told me to try again, but to try with my heart, to let my heart talk and not my mouth. That night, after everyone was in bed, I began to run a hot bath and try to read my Bible. I began to pray. I started to pray like I usually did, as though God was a genie who granted wishes. "Dear God, I need you to do A, B, C, and D. Please forgive me for my sins. Amen." I hear Pa in my head, telling me to speak from my heart. I begin by telling him I'm angry with him. Why did you desert me? What did I ever do to deserve what I have been through? I even had the stupid audacity to scream at him that he owed ME for not deserting HIM, and I threw my Bible across the bathroom floor.

The Holy Spirit checked me real fast. He spoke to me and told me Jesus had saved me, not because I deserved it but because God was merciful; that no matter what I ever did, I could never repay him — not that he asked for it, but if I was going to keep score, I had better keep the right score. He knew I was angry and had been waiting for me to surrender to him. I turn off my bath water, and I'm standing in the middle of my bathroom naked, both physically and emotionally. I screamed at God from the bottom of my soul. Why?!?!? What more do you want from me? Where are you? You said you would always be there, but where are you?!? I fell to my knees on my bathroom floor, and I started crying uncontrollably. I need you,

Father! I am helpless and I'm frightened. My children are sick. They are innocent. They are hurting. Don't you care?!

I prayed from the depths of my heart and soul. I prayed from the depths of the despair I was in. I yell to God, "Here I am, broken and begging for you to tell me what to do… tell me what to do!" My screams turn into a normal tone and then eventually sobs. Broken, whimpering sobs. I lay crumbled on the floor. I can feel the coolness of the tile against my skin. I have no more words, but there is so much my soul wants to say. My heart and soul begin crying out to God; the Holy Spirit intercedes for me. My spirit lay shattered in a million pieces all around me, like a suit of armor that had disintegrated into small pieces and scattered all around me. I'm lying there completely raw and exposed; the façade, the wall I had put up, has crumbled around me. I'm vulnerable and stripped bare, to the very heart of me. God tells me to pick up my copy of The Word of God.

I picked up my Bible, and there was the story of Job. I put on my robe and began reading right there on my bathroom floor. I read the entire book through my tears, and I understood. For the first time in a long time, I knew what to do. I could feel God all around me. I could feel his comfort like a warm embrace. I surrendered all control. I gave it all to God. As I finished praying, a peace came over me that literally breathed life into me like CPR. I took a huge breath of air of that God created air. It was the first time I could breathe in years. From that point on, I gave it all to him. If I was afraid, I looked to him. If I was scared, angry, hurt, or happy, I looked to him. I trusted in him, and I had faith in him with full surrender. Not faith in my will, but in his. I trusted that whatever he wanted would be for the best, and I prayed for HIS will to be done, not mine.

My family and I started attending church regularly. We tithed what little money we had. Our family as a whole had surrendered. All four of our children gave their hearts and devotion to Christ. That summer, my husband and our three oldest children were all baptized. The following year, our youngest daughter was baptized. God gave us the Job season to strip us down so that He could rebuild us for His purpose and calling on our lives. He loved us too much to have a superficial relationship with him. The more I gave it to God, the more peace He gave me. God made it all better.

He didn't heal my children, but he healed our spirits. They will have their diseases until the day they get their resurrected bodies. God did give us answers, though. Our oldest son suffers from a rare disease called Hyper-IGE syndrome aka Job's Disease.(How fitting is that?!) His bone marrow makes too many immunoglobulin E cells; these are particular types of antibodies that your immune system releases against allergens. His disease causes boils and cysts, frequent lung infections, and damage to his spine and his organs, like the spleen and liver. He will still need a bone marrow transplant at some point, but for now we can manage it and his quality of life has drastically improved. Our youngest daughter has a rare disease, a similar disease to our son, a sister disease if you will. (No pun intended) . She has hyper-IGD syndrome (HIDS/MVK), which means her body makes too many immunoglobulin D cells. They are the primary infection-fighting antibodies. Her disease causes high fevers, joint pain and stiffness, a rash, headaches, and stomach pain. Both of them also have a ridiculously rare second disease: they both have CAPS disease, just different versions. Our son has the FCAS version and our youngest daughter has the MWS version. Cold air triggers their bodies, causing flare-ups and pain. Our youngest still has flare-ups, but we have learned how to manage them better and they don't happen nearly as often.

Our oldest daughter has a rare adrenal gland disease called Addison's disease. Her adrenal gland doesn't produce enough of the hormones called cortisol and aldosterone. It causes a lack of salt, severely low blood pressure, kidney issues, joint pain, stomach pain, dry skin and hair, and darkening of the skin in spots. She also has hypothyroidism and Tourette's. She now takes medicine and keeps a salty drink with her at all times. She still struggles some days, but it is manageable. Our middle daughter still has epilepsy and the side effects of a TBI, but she now has a cat that alerts her when she needs to rest or her anxiety is too high, in order to prevent a seizure. He also alerts me, especially in the middle of the night, if she does have a seizure, giving us the freedom to get a restful night of sleep. She doesn't need therapy or medicine to control her seizures or anxiety; just her best friend... her cat. She is slowly coming out of her shell, and I can see her older self slowly returning.

We found our way through home school and navigating the waters became a lot easier. God used their ill-will for our good. When COVID happened, nothing changed for us regarding their education. My children didn't suffer from closed schools or disrupted lives. Nor are they corrupted by the curriculum that is coming out of some schools today. We get to dive deep into subjects that will help them towards their dream careers. If they are struggling in a particular lesson or subject, we can slow down and ensure they understand and retain the lesson before progressing. While it will never be OK regarding what led us to homeschool our children, I am eternally grateful God had greater plans for us.

My husband and I are inseparable, and I laugh again. I find joy and laughter daily in my marriage. My spirit is strong and my soul is on fire. God didn't miraculously heal my children; he healed my spirit and my resolve. I see all those times I cried out, "Where are you?" — he was there all along. All those times I screamed at him, I blamed him, and I accused him of turning his back on me...he was right there. He loved me in spite of it. The night our oldest daughter passed out, she was in an addisonian crisis, but we didn't know it. She could have died, but God was watching over her. Our oldest could be in a hospital on chemo for his bone marrow, his spleen could have ruptured, or his lung could have completely blown out, but all those times, God was watching over him. All those fevers that were dangerously high—just a few more degrees, and the doctors said they could have caused brain damage to our youngest or killed her, but instead God was watching over her. Our middle daughter suffered a brain injury that could have killed her or left her severely damaged from hitting her temple; instead, God was watching over her. We could have lost our home and filed bankruptcy, but God was watching over us and provided exactly what we needed to survive. Our marriage could have been broken; we could have forever drawn apart; instead, God was watching over us and ensured our marriage stayed strong. I rejoice in the depth of the hardships because I know God is doing great things in our perseverance.

If this has been a hard year or season for you, if you feel broken, or your soul is tired. Please don't have another moment with the same defeated heart. Go to the Lord with a renewed hope, because the same God that created the universe, the same father that controls the sun and the moon, has the same power to give you comfort and joy. He has the power to control the situation, he is faithful, he will never abandon you. I know the pain you feel, the desperation, and the desire to quit. But I also know that sometimes you have to hit rock bottom, so you will look up from the depths of the pit to see God's glorious hand reaching to pull you out. Sometimes God puts mountains in our path, not to cause us to stumble but to show you that, with him, mountains can be moved. Having Christ in your heart doesn't mean tough times won't happen to you, or that you will never experience heartache or loss. It does mean you'll never experience it alone. You'll never travel this journey without someone having your back, without someone loving you and guiding you even when you're angry with him. Even when you are so broken, you feel dead inside. He restores my soul, and you will be amazed at what a Spirit on Fire can do. I hope everyone finds the comfort and grace of God. Don't give up; reach up; God's hand is always stretched out waiting for you to grab hold!

Refined Silver

So we do not lose heart. Though our outer self is wasting away, our inner self is being renewed day by day. For this light momentary affliction is preparing for us an eternal weight of glory beyond all comparison, as we look not to the things that are seen but to the things that are unseen. For the things that are seen are transient, but the things that are unseen are eternal.

2nd Corinthians 4:16-18

~ 18 ~

I was 15 years old when I first felt pins and needles running down my arms. It would come and go sporadically, like the numbness you get when you have slept on your arm too long, inconvenient but not enough to hinder my daily activity. Then, at 16 years old, I started experiencing the weirdest sensation when I would turn my head. I would suddenly feel a burning sensation run down my neck and into my right arm. It felt like my blood was on fire and was pouring down my neck like an internal river of lava. It would get so hot, you could physically feel the heat on the outside of my skin along the path to my arm. It wasn't painful, just incredibly hot and uncomfortable. I assumed it happened because I turned my neck the wrong way, thus temporarily pinching a nerve. I should have known something was off then, but I didn't. It wasn't until I experienced a massive flare-up after giving birth to our middle daughter that I discovered something wasn't right neurologically.

I was one week postpartum when suddenly I had crippling pain in my arms and legs that was accompanied by tightness around my chest. It felt as though a boa constrictor was wrapped around my torso, squeezing the breath out of me. I suddenly couldn't walk and was so fatigued that I struggled to stay awake even after I slept for 12 hours. My husband had to physically help carry me into the doctor's office because my legs buckled underneath me. After running blood tests for diseases that included my symptoms, such as lupus and Lyme disease, the doctor diagnosed me with fibromyalgia. He explained that fibromyalgia had become the catch-all disease; if one couldn't figure out what type of chronic illness disease they had, fibromyalgia was the answer.

Over the next 10 years, I slowly got worse with each episode until I was experiencing the same symptoms such as pain and fatigue every single day. I went to the doctor every 3 months, and every 3 months, I would complain that it seemed to be getting worse. They would tell me I was depressed and that my pain and sleeping all the time were symptoms of depression. No matter how much I explained that I wasn't depressed, doctors insisted I had to be based on my childhood. They were certain I had fibromyalgia coupled with depression-so much so, they couldn't see the forest for the trees. Some doctors would act like it was all in my head and that I was manifesting the pain. Or worse, that I only wanted pain medication, even though one look at my chart would show that I've refused pain medication since the very beginning.

Every time a new issue would arise, they would always come up with a simple explanation and dismiss discussion of any other explanation. I would easily become overheated in the summer, causing dizziness and severe fatigue. Doctors passed it off as a side effect of being in the sun after taking my medication, even though the sun didn't bother me in the cold months. My joints would ache and stiffen as though I were the Tin Man from The Wizard of Oz and in need of oil, but I was told it was arthritis, even though I was in my 20s. I felt like I needed to pee all the time, but I could only pee in small amounts at a time, so I had to use the bathroom 4-6 times an hour, every hour of the day and night. I was told it was I.C. bladder disease, a by-product of my hysterectomy. I had severely sharp pain and blurriness in my eyes, only to be told I must have migraines and just not be aware of them. I would complain of the sheer fatigue I experienced every day. Their answer? Depression, of course. I complained of the increasing pains in my limbs every night and the insomnia that I struggled with.

Along with brain fog and struggling to remember words as I went through the day in a haze. They reiterated that it was fibromyalgia. Every new complication was met with an easy fix, yet nothing was fixed, and I was continuing to feel worse. It had gotten so bad that I would have to take a nap before picking the children up from school, and by the time I had gotten back to my house, which is 10 miles away, I would be so fatigued I could barely get out of the vehicle and into the house before falling asleep. At every doctor's appointment, I had to fight with my doctors to listen to me. They would pretend to listen, but then tell me what I was describing couldn't possibly be. I knew my own body better than they did; after all, I have lived with it my entire life. That didn't matter; I didn't have an M.D. after my name, so I was to fall in line and stop questioning the diagnosis.

Everything changed in the fall of 2019 because of a bologna sandwich, of all things. I was eating a bologna sandwich with mustard and onions (that's the only way to eat a bologna sandwich, for the record). I unknowingly bit down, and then, out of nowhere, I was zapped with a lightning bolt that shot across the left side of my face. It burned like the flames of hell as the electric shock ran across my face. It felt like the hand of God physically reached down and touched my face, bringing me to my knees. Lighting burned all the way to my bottom teeth along my jaw. It ran up to my eye and felt like I was being stabbed with a hot ice pick through the middle of my eye. The intensity of the pain in my forehead caused me to instinctively cradle my head as though it were about to explode. It spread along my cheek and nose as if the lightning was trying to escape my face and shoot out my nose. It only lasted seconds, yet the pain was so intolerable, those seconds seemed like a lifetime.

Refined Silver

I have a very high pain tolerance, yet this brush with the hand of God, a lightning bolt, brought me to my knees. I could do nothing but roll around on the floor, groaning in pain as the shocking, burning, and electrical pain seared my face. I thought it was an exposed root in one of my teeth since it lit up all my teeth the moment I bit down on the sandwich. As soon as I recovered, I was standing in my dentist's office. I was diagnosed with trigeminal neuralgia, aka, the most excruciating pain known to humanity in the medical community. I can testify to the validity of their hypothesis as I have never felt anything as agonizing as what I went through! Ever! The trigeminal nerve runs from your ear and branches to your forehead, across your cheek, and to your jaw bone. Trigeminal neuralgia is when that nerve is triggered, causing the most horrendous burning electric sensation. The slightest touch of the cheek can trigger it, as can chewing too much or even a slight cool breeze.

They put me on medication, and I immediately changed my lifestyle to reduce the frequency of the attacks. I quit smoking; I no longer chew gum, jerky, or anything that requires a lot of chewing. To reduce the number of times I touch my face, I wear the bare minimum of makeup most days, rather than a full face of makeup as I used to. I even keep an umbrella in my truck, not so much for rainy days but mainly for severely windy days. I cannot begin to help you understand just how truly painful it is. Even if you thought of the worst pain you ever felt in your life and multiplied it by 100, it still wouldn't be in the same category. (All my trigeminal neuralgia sufferers are nodding their heads in agreement.)

One positive thing that came from this horrendously painful disease was finally getting an MRI. It's rare for someone in their 30s to have trigeminal neuralgia. Those that do usually have Multiple Sclerosis (MS) as well. The neurologist finally did the MRI, and sure enough, I had lesions in my spine and brain. I had Multiple Sclerosis; I had suffered with it for over a decade, undiagnosed. It was a scary diagnosis, but I was more relieved than anything. I finally had an answer, proof in black and white... it wasn't in my head. Well, physically it was, but not in the way that all of those previous doctors had determined. As I look back at all of those doctor appointments and all of my symptoms, the writing has always been on the wall. No one bothered to put it together or order an MRI.

MS is a disease in which the immune system attacks the protective sheath (myelin) that covers the nerves, causing communication problems between the brain and the rest of your body. Eventually, the disease causes permanent damage or deterioration of the nerves. MS is a snowflake disease, meaning no two are alike, which is partly why it's so hard to finally get a diagnosis. I can only speak to my personal experience living with MS; others' experiences and symptoms can be different. I think most people either forget that or maybe they just don't know that everyone is different. When people find out that I have MS, it never fails to hear the inevitable, "I know Jim Bob he has MS; and can't walk at all. You must have a mild case." Or "My Aunt Susan has MS, and she swears by this super secret natural remedy that came from the belly of an extinct dinosaur found in the deep caves of Atlantis." As well as the most offensive and irritating one, "Wow, you don't look sick." If you have said any of these, I say this out of love...stop it! Chronic illness patients have seen multiple doctors and have done as much research as they can before agreeing on a treatment plan with their doctor. People with chronic illness often do not "look sick."

Just because we may carry or, in some cases, hide the weight of the disease well, doesn't mean it isn't heavy. There is SO much that people don't see. Most people don't see the days when the pain is so severe, I can't even get out of bed. They don't see me chug the energy drink right after a nap so that I can be awake and attend their baby shower, child's birthday party, or small group. They don't see my husband physically carry me into our house because I spent all of my energy serving others. They don't see the incessant itching over my entire body as my nerves are creating white static that feels like spiders are crawling all over me. My family is the only one who gets to see the ugly truth of how MS looks on me. I am extremely blessed because the disease is so hard for me that without God's intervening, I would fail at most things. Daily, I see God show up faithfully. He gives me purpose and his grace sustains me.

For a control freak like me, it's easy to try to fix things myself instead of giving everything over to God. With MS, my own body is in many ways out of my control. It keeps my need for God in complete focus at all times. In order for you to see what God does daily in my walk with MS, I have to walk you through what I experience every day with my chronic illness. I haven't had a single day without pain in all 4 of my limbs in over a decade. Not a single day. Because substance abuse and addiction run on both sides of my family, I refuse to take narcotics stronger than Tramadol. Due to having a 70-80% genetic risk of breast cancer, I cannot take medication to help reduce the symptoms or flare-ups as they increase the risk of breast cancer. Only God, Jesus, the Holy Spirit, and my family get me through each day without giving up. I have the beautiful advantage of seeing God do miraculous things for me. Even in my suffering, God has helped me ensure that I show up for my mission of pursuing those far from God to lead them to Jesus. I have had to learn how to prioritize things, but I have only had to cancel on obligations less than a handful of times in a decade. That is all God, and is miraculous by itself, especially for someone living with chronic illness .

Refined Silver

Even when I'm not in a flare-up, my body experiences symptoms. I have lost strength in my muscles to the point where even a gallon of milk seems quite heavy some days. My muscles fatigue easily. Just walking around the mall can cause my legs to be so weak and shake so badly that I need help even sitting down and getting up from the dinner table that evening. I am chair-or-bed-bound the next day as I recover. Some days, my cognitive problems leave me disoriented and walking around in a haze as though I have had a couple of beers. I can function, but I'm in a tipsy state where my perception is off. There are times I can't form thoughts or sentences, while on other days, words elude me. I know that I know the word I am searching for, but it's tucked away in the file cabinet of my mind. A file cabinet I cannot get opened on my own. My brain will give me just enough to describe it so that someone else can help me find the word with prompting. For example, if you gave me the word "nail polish," I may not be able to remember what it's called, but I know what it means, and I can describe it. Such as, "What do you call the colored stuff that you paint on your fingernails?" There are times when my brain will give me the wrong word, such as compartment instead of component. Or laundry soap when I'm needing the words dish soap.

In spite of it all, God has given me the words needed to write this book. He gives me the ability to do motivational speaking engagements without blundering, but the moment I step off stage away from the public eye, my brain will go back to glitching. At home, my family knows me so well that we have our own language. They call it "Brandy-isms," where I combine words or meanings or just butcher the English language all together. Most of the time, they know what I'm thinking or needing without me even saying it, and they are patient with me on days I fumble every word. I will never forget or need reminding of how loving God and my family are, because I get to see God's grace and my family's heart for me every day through my struggles.

I have lost almost all feeling in my limbs and torso. If I press hard enough, I can feel the pressure, but it is diluted and delayed. I rarely feel hot or cold temperatures in my hands, mouth, or upper chest. If the temperature is really hot or really cold, my brain will register the temperature after a delayed period of time. That may not appear to be a big deal, but when you lose most of your sense of touch, you end up hurting yourself without realizing it. I have suffered burns on my hands and chest from scalding water, hot steam, hot pans, or piping hot food. As well as ice burns from holding something frozen for too long. My biggest issues are mobility, stiffness, and pain in my limbs and neck. I'm not sure how I've lost most of the feeling in these places, but I can feel deep aches and pain all the time. The best way I can describe it is; if you have ever had a broken bone, you know that deep ache in your bone as it heals?

Take that and add it to the numb yet painful tingling you feel when your foot goes to sleep. Add that to how heavy your arms or legs feel when you wrap a weighted bag around your ankles or wrists. That's how it feels all the time.

I experience muscle spasms or twitching often, even with medicine to reduce the severity. They range from Charlie Horse feeling to a fluttering in that body part where my muscle twitches so strongly that you can see it with your naked eye. My eyes and thigh muscles are usually the more common body parts in which I experience twitching. Sometimes, I may also have a stabbing or shooting pain, or sometimes I lose all feeling as if my legs are suddenly gone. I will have to look and feel them to convince my brain that my legs are still there. I think this phenomenon is my brain's wishful thinking of a reprieve from the pain. Some days, they are stiff and incredibly hard to bend, and it is difficult to lift my feet off the ground. I'm pretty sure the Tin Man in The Wizard of Oz has MS because he can't move his limbs until they are oiled, and even then he walks straight-legged. Because that's exactly what it's like. Not only is it hard to walk, bend, or get up and down, it's incredibly painful.

When the pain gets too severe and I contemplate chopping off my limbs, I pray for relief or strength to persevere. God always gives me what I need. There are some nights when I lie in bed crying from the pain and just talk to God through my heartache, and instantly the pain subsides from a 10 to a 4. I am blessed with the daily reminder that my God is still in control; he doesn't sit on the sidelines, and he hasn't forsaken me! I always joke that I have the bladder of a 90-year-old because I have to pee 60 times a day, often causing me to abruptly excuse myself from a conversation or meeting because I have to pee again… even though I had just peed 15 minutes before. Bless my family's hearts, road trips are torture for them because I add hours to our trip just from constantly having to stop at a gas station. It doesn't matter how little fluid I drink that day. My bladder is a magical pitcher that never runs dry. In order to be present during our 1-hour church service, I have to pee right before leaving the house, even though we are only going 15 minutes down the road. Once I get there, I pee again and then another time right before church starts. Then as soon as service is over, I have to pee again, and the moment I walk back in the door at our house, you guessed....have to pee again.

Out of all my issues, fatigue is the hardest to live with because there is more sleeping than living. Not to brag, but I make Sleeping Beauty look rested. It's not your typical "I'm tired and need a cup of coffee" fatigue. This type is, out of nowhere, battery depleted, can't take another step, like "you have never slept a day in your life." (You read that in the rhythm of a Nyquil commercial, didn't you?) The kind that a good night's sleep or nap can't fix. Just walking to your bed when you're suddenly exhausted is like walking through quicksand and up a mountain.

Thankfully, God has blessed me with an internal warning system: about 30 minutes before I am so drained I can't walk, my body will begin to shake, similar to when your blood sugar drops. When that happens, I know that I have a very short window to lie down and sleep before I crash. If I do not get to lie down and sleep, my body will suddenly power down, and I will have a temporary flare-up. If this happens, I can no longer walk or talk; I struggle to move my arms or legs; and my eyes start to lose vision until I sleep. I usually end up sleeping 4 to 5 hours at a minimum when this happens, regardless of whether it's 10 a.m. or 8 p.m. There is no rhyme or reason to when and how fatigue strikes. I can paint an entire house and still feel energized without being depleted.

However, a quick trip to the grocery store or a couple hours of work on the computer could drain me for the entire day. Every day is an adventure because I don't know what it will bring. It keeps me humble and never in danger of forgetting I can do nothing outside of Christ because I physically cannot do anything without God's provisions for that day. There are days that I cope with everything more easily than other days. Then, there are days I want to lash out and scream that I've had enough. That it's too much.

That it's not fair. I want to say "why me" and "I don't deserve this." Mostly, I want to scream that I give up. Those moments are when I see Christ offer me the most grace and mercy. He meets me as I'm crying in the tub or withering in pain in the recliner, trying to get relief.

He knows my suffering firsthand; he knows my pain, he knows my utter exhaustion, and he knows when I need to be reminded of his love for me. The thing with a chronic illness is that you can't give up. This isn't a movie you can walk out of. It's not a race you can cut short. It doesn't stop because you want it to stop. So after you've had your bad day, you give yourself the grace to have a moment of weakness and self-pity. Then you do what you always do: you turn to God to pick you up, and you try to make the most of your life. You keep repeating this process over and over again. It's OK if your illness wears you down sometimes; it's expected. It's what you do after it knocks you down that matters. You can't do it alone. You have to depend on your family and friends. I can't imagine not having my family's help and support. We get so wrapped up in day-to-day life that we sometimes take our close circle for granted. Thankfully, God has blessed me with this disease, and I am ever aware of my family's support and sacrifice for me.

One of the greatest shows of love from my husband and son was during a spastic moment. I was struggling

Refined Silver

under the weight of MS. I could barely lift my right leg off the ground. My foot dragged the floor when I walked, and my knee would barely bend. I knew it would be hard, but I knew church was where I needed to be. At the end of the service, I went and got on my knees in front of the alter. I just cried as I sat in the presence of God. I needed him, and I needed his reminder that he would get me through it. When I no sooner than said Amen and wondered how I was going to get off the floor, I felt my husband on one side of me and my son on the other. Without so much as a word, I felt them tenderly put an arm under each of my arms and scoop me up. They walked/carried me back to my seat without so much as a word. The entire congregation was still standing and worshipping, and I wanted to stand but was so exhausted from pouring out my soul at the alter. Once again, without so much as a word, they instinctively knew my heart and held up on either side. We stood there, their arms interlocked with mine, holding me upright, and we worshipped and praised our God-head together.

My girls will take it upon themselves to clean the house or do the laundry when they see I'm having a bad day. They will come cuddle with me in bed and read me a story when I'm bed-bound. They have ran a soaking bath for me and helped me get undressed without me even asking, knowing I can barely move and that I will need help. My disease has blessed me with seeing my family as the light of my life on the darkest of my days. They pour into me as much as I pour into them. Some days I have massive amounts of mom guilt. Instead of listing off all the sacrifices our family has made because of MS, they offer grace, love, and reassurance. Even with the best support systems, it's not enough without Christ, as the waves of symptoms will try to drown you. Praise God! Jesus has the ultimate power and control over the raging waves! Matthew 8:26: And he said to them, "Why are you afraid, O you of little faith?" Then he rose and rebuked the winds and the sea, and there was a great calm. There are days when I feel like giving up, and I cry to the Lord to please just give me a reprieve from the pain or fatigue for just 5 minutes so that I can strengthen myself. On days where the weight is so heavy, I just sit in the presence of God and ask him to help carry the load for a bit.

There are days when I say nothing at all when I pray. I just cry and let my heart and tears do the talking. These last few months have been incredibly hard, both physically and emotionally. I find myself speaking less and sleeping more, but above all, I praise Christ all day and night. For one day, I will be in my resurrected body, a perfect and pain-free body. I will be whole and in God's presence all because Christ saved me and offered me redemption. Eternal glory with God is worth every second of hell I experience on Earth. I praise him for giving me this burden, because it has deepened my dependence on God and relationship with Christ and the Holy Spirit. When I'm drowning, THE ONE

Refined Silver

who can calm the seas calls me his. I hear his voice as I look over the thrashing waves and see Jesus walking on water, reaching out his hand to me! Jesus, the one who with a mere whisper on his lips can bring things into creation, perform miracles, make old into new, revive your spirit, relieve your pain, wipe your tears, comfort you, and put you back together again...calls me by name!

Refined Silver

"You have heard that it was said, 'Love your neighbor and hate your enemy. But I tell you, love your enemies and pray for those who persecute you, that you may be children of your Father in heaven. He causes his sun to rise on the evil and the good, and sends rain on the righteous and the unrighteous. If you love those who love you, what reward will you get? Are not even the tax collectors doing that? And if you greet only your own people, what are you doing more than others? Do not even pagans do that? Be perfect, therefore, as your heavenly Father is perfect".

Matthew 5:43-48

Refined Silver

~ 19 ~

It all started when my son turned 16 and broke his mama's heart because he was almost an adult. At least that's what I tell him when we discuss 2020. The day he turned 16, COVID hit our community, and hit it hard. Within a week, some of our most godly and wise brothers and sisters in Christ were in the hospital on a ventilator, slowly losing their lives. As a family with health problems, this brand new and lethal virus that seemed to appear out of nowhere was concerning, to say the least. We hunkered down, washed our gallons of milk, and bathed in sanitizer. Looking back I feel foolish, to have been so easily led by fear. In my defense, every day there was conflicting data, and every day we were fed fear by the media. It wasn't many years before, when a single Epstein-Barr Virus all but tried to kill us, and Covid was to be more fatal. Of course, I freaked out, that's the human response…not the Christ-like one. How easy it is for the shadows of our trauma, to cripple us when we focus on the shadows more than Christ.

By the end of the month, the country would be shut down for "14 days" in order to "flatten the curve." I have thoughts on the virus and our response as a nation; our response as Christ's Church; and how it was weaponized to be a quiver in the political bow. I will keep my thoughts and opinions mostly to myself. However, I will say one thing, having lost my father-in-law to the virus. I loved that man beyond words, a man who called me his daughter and loved me immensely. A man who is still painfully missed every single day! Losing him in the manner we did and not being allowed to see him is a tragedy that should never have happened. It should be criminal that families early over the world were robbed of their final goodbyes while our loved ones died alone. Over a virus that had a 99% survival rate. My children were never allowed to see their grandfather, and they were never allowed to say goodbye. While he is joyfully waiting for us in heaven, my children will live the remainder of their lives with this deep heartache and regret because our hospitals allowed fear to overthrow reason. It should be criminal that this virus was made and altered in a lab and then released, either intentionally or unintentionally.

From the beginning of the virus into the summer, my husband transported P.P.E. and COVID tests to hospitals and doctors' offices all over the state so that they would have the resources to save lives. Our state was still in lockdown mode. Churches and schools were still closed; grocery store shelves were still bare; and first responders and the medical community were heroes. Summer came, and everything changed in the blink of an eye. My husband has been blessed with an abundance of training and expertise in specialty areas that most in law enforcement are rarely afforded the opportunity to have. As a result, he has been given once-in-a-lifetime opportunities that many of us will never have. Such as standing on the sidelines at the Super Bowl watching the Patriots decimate the Rams. Or standing on the sidelines at the SEC championship bowl as the Georgia Bulldogs rematched Auburn and claimed their title. He has been on dignitary details for security when royals and politicians from around the world come to our state to visit. Including presidential details whenever the leaders from the highest office in the land came to Georgia, including but not limited to President Trump and Vice President Pence. Most of these opportunities, our family unfortunately weren't able to participate in with him. However, at the end of May that year, our family was gifted with the opportunity to explore the motorcade of the President and Vice President and hang out with their private Secret Services detail since my husband was also a lead car on the detail the following day. The dichotomy of being in the private hangar, taking pictures of the motorcade, and the following night seeing my husband under attack is so starkly different, they could be from two different countries.

The summer riots of 2020 are unlike anything our country has ever seen. Our family had been through riots before, but nothing like what we experienced in 2020. My husband stood at the front lines in Atlanta during Ferguson, St. Louis, Baltimore, and every other protest. Those were child's play compared to the Atlanta and other major city riots in 2020. In this one, they were militarized, organized, and paid for. I don't know who funded them or trained them, but make no mistake about it, they were heavily trained and heavily funded. They were bussed in from all over the country with their weapons, lodging, and needs already paid for before they ever took a step off the bus. My husband had to drive throughout the city and look for pallets of bricks that the BLM and Antifa organizations had magically delivered. Regardless of what politicians tell you, both BLM and Antifa are organizations. They aren't just mere ideologies. They are communist and socialist ideologies formed into chapters (groups) that branch off of one central hub. They are domestic terrorist groups that are brought in to create havoc and chaos purely for political unrest under the guise of social justice.

My husband stood on the front lines every night for weeks, being pelted with rocks bigger than your hand, bricks, and chunks of concrete. He and the other law enforcement officers were spit on, and bombed with Molotov cocktails and high-grade fireworks. They had knives and razor blades thrown at them; one night, a rioter even tried to cut my husband with a chainsaw. The BLM rioters didn't care that my husband is a good, honest, and Godly man who fought daily for 18 years to bring true change and reform to communities, as does most every other law enforcement officer. They didn't care about their fellow rioter who was handcuffed in the backseat of a police car as the rioters set it on fire with him in the backseat either. My husband and other officers were the ones who risked their lives and pulled the man out of the burning car, not the rioters. All they cared about was destruction and hatred in their hearts toward law enforcement. They were armed with the Marxist playbook and had been paid to wage war in our streets. Atlanta and other major cities around the nation became war zones, and law enforcement was their #1 target.

Before I continue with the events of that summer and how this round in the fire might have been the hardest one for our family yet. I want to pause and have an honest discussion about the dangers of the worldview of critical race and Marxism, the mantras of BLM. As a Christian, it is fundamentally imperative that the Word of God be written on our hearts so that we may not be deceived. I have witnessed Christ's church have good intentions but disastrous consequences by aligning themselves with BLM. Every Christian should value all life regardless of age, ethnicity, status, race, gender, or creed. We are all made in the image of our Father, thus, we all hold intrinsic value! That doesn't mean Christianity should be baptized into the "Woke" movement of Black Lives Matter, whose worldview is rooted in Marxism. One glance at the BLM website tells you their agenda: they want to gain power to change power structures in the halls of American politics and beyond. This woke justice system has mortally wounded our nation. Negatively impacted businesses, and now it has infused into evangelism. The modern social justice agenda is not about equality and civil rights; it is about disrupting systems and gaining systems of power in order to achieve their progressive political agendas. We are told that if you do not accept this social justice, it is tantamount to sacrificing puppies, that you are not a true Christian, but I would argue that Christians cannot accept their social justice. BLM is built on a postmodern foundation with the goal of destruction and disruption. Their key beliefs and goals fundamentally oppose Christianity and our doctrine on essential issues such as human sexuality, ethnic prejudice, marriage, family construct and social engagement. All the things, that God himself created for HIS glory.

BLM has become more than a "movement"; it is now a religion, a religion of social justice and not Christ's gospel. We have witnessed white people all over the nation being forced to bow and repent of their inherent white sins to the god of social justice to engage in virtue signaling. It is no different than ancient Jews bowing down to Greek gods in order to live and trade with the Romans. Its gospel is a social gospel and not the gospel of Jesus Christ. The doctrine and principles of Marxism and BLM do not align with the doctrine of Christ. You cannot have one foot in Christianity and one foot in the world view of Marxism. They are fundamentally and equivocally opposed to each other.

Although Galatians 1:8-9 warns us not to be deceived, many in our country have foolishly embraced the godless anti-gospel message of BLM in their grief over injustice. But, Jesus Christ is the only unifier, not social justice, BLM, or politics. He takes people, regardless of their gender or ethnic distinction—those who are in many ways opposed to one another—and brings us into a familial bond where we are brothers and sisters through the blood of Christ. Only He can lead communities to peace, love, and unity. Marxism and Christianity cannot co-exist; they cannot correspond; they are diabolically opposed to one another. Marxism, and its current version in BLM, is unbiblical. In Marxism, there is no God; man has no soul; he is the property and slave of a totalitarian state. In Christianity, man is reconciled with the One True Living God and given eternal life through Christ. To be free of the oppression of sin, man must freely give all of himself to Christ. He is solely responsible to God, Jesus, and the Holy Spirit and surrenders fully in proper alignment, knowing that man is inherently depraved and God is the Creator, the only who gives and takes away, and the only one who rules and reigns over man outside of the construct of time and space forever.

We should be grieved by injustice; we should call out sin for sin; we should not turn a blind eye to the suffering, but we do so according to the Word of God. We spread the gospel of Christ and live our lives aligned with the rule and reign of God. We don't cave to the gods of social justice or topple systems of power to raise up another group that will oppress the former.

Shew, we now return to our previously scheduled programming. (It makes me sad that newer generations did not hear the movie announcer's voice in their head when they read that just now.) My husband, along with many other law enforcement officers and State Troopers, held down the front lines for 12-16 hours straight, every night for over a month. Progressive politicians tied their hands behind their backs and sent them out to be beaten and battered. They were instructed to not engage, but to retreat when need be. Rioters and criminals were given keys to the city of Atlanta and were given free range to burn, loot, and destroy whatever they chose. During the daytime, when the mayor had to pretend the city was safe for Corporate America, my husband and other agencies were told to arrest them, give them a desk appearance ticket, and let them go. The city of Atlanta brought buses in. The officers and state troopers would place the disruptive protestors in zip ties and walk them onto the detainment bus. Where they would receive an appearance ticket, then law enforcement would cut off the zip ties and literally walked out the back of the bus to be allowed to riot in the streets at night. Some rioters had been arrested 4 or 5 times in a single day or night and were still in the streets. Rioters broke into the Georgia State Patrol building and threw Molotov cocktails into the dispatch room, trying to set state troopers and dispatchers on fire. My husband came home one night with the soles of his shoes scorched and burned to the point where the rubber soles had come apart.

My husband seemed to age over night, with the stress shown on his face and the heartache in his eyes. He was surrounded by hate and called every name in the book. They would stand in his face and tell him the monstrosities they wanted to do to us, his wife, and children. They took pictures of his face and badge and doxed our families. My daughters and I received messages from strangers telling us they were coming to our house to rape us. They would threaten to cut our heads off or hang us in the front yard. We had to have our property information hidden on county records; we had to temporarily change our names and hunker down in hiding. Was my husband an evil person who committed unspeakable atrocities, was he a menace to our country? No, he just answered a call from God to protect and serve our state. Because he was a white man and in law enforcement, the two most hated and dangerous qualifiers for those on the left, he was deemed a threat.

Refined Silver

How I would log onto social media, and see misguided people from my church call us racists and that the system my family sacrificed for needed to be overthrown. The people who knew us... the very people my husband served alongside on Sundays, who he watched over and protected... called him the problem. They virtue signaled and changed their pictures to little black boxes, and they repeated the mythical lie of systemic racism in law enforcement. They donated their money to the BLM cause and patted themselves on the back for a job well done. All the while my husband and his brothers and sisters in blue, 30 minutes away, were under attack. The media called us Nazis; they falsely told the world we, the thin blue line, were dangerous and were targeting black men to unjustly kill them. The media and vocal celebrities were quick to dismiss factual statics and evidence that this was a false narrative.

Even my children couldn't be shielded from the vitriol as Disney and Nickelodeon ran anti-law enforcement and pro-BLM public service announcements. Fellow law enforcement officers were followed home and their cars were set on fire in their driveways. Nowhere was safe, not the grocery store or gas station, not our homes or even our church. A place that was supposed to be our refuge had been politicized by some of its members; they too fanned the flames that were burning us.

Refined Silver

On the night of June 13th, it went from bad to worse. The night rioters burned a Wendy's in Atlanta to the ground. My husband and three other troopers found themselves unsuspectingly surrounded by over 1,000 rioters. Help was coming, but it took far too long as other law enforcement tried to clear a pathway, under the bloodthirsty eyes of the Mayor and D.A. of Atlanta. The very people who had tied my husband and others' hands, painted a target on their back and then jailed them for doing their jobs. All the while, my husband and the other three troopers were sitting ducks, caught without their riot gear. They are pelted with concrete pieces from the roadway. They have been backed up against a hillside by the overpass. They are desperately trying to duck and dodge the bottles of urine and feces being thrown at them and the fiery Molotov cocktails being lobbed at them. Some make contact, some don't.

In the melee of the attack, my husband was injured at the base of his spine, but the adrenaline of everything prevented his body from registering what had happened. It wasn't until they finally had backup did he realize he couldn't feel his legs due to numbness. He pushed it out of his mind, thinking it's just fatigue from standing on the concrete jungle floor for 12 or more hours a night for the last month. It wasn't until the next morning, when he experienced agonizing pain in his back and numbness in his legs, that he realized his injury was serious.

An MRI revealed severe damage from L2 all the way to S1 in his spine. Some discs had been completely blown out and the vertebras were now curved into each other; some were bulging due to the stress of those disks futilely trying to uphold the weight of the spine. His spine was now and forever 11° out of balance and severely mangled. They told us that one wrong move or blow to his spine could forever paralyze him. He was forced to retire at 18 years and 1 day after being classified as having a Special Line of Duty injury, a classification for an injury sustained during a felonious assault.

We lost our life insurance and our vision insurance because my husband was 35 and in order to keep those when you retired, you had to be 55 years of age. His retirement was a percentage of his yearly salary. Ask any law enforcement family; they can tell you, it's not a lot unless you work a lot of off duty. Our income went from six figures a year if you combined off duty to less than $50,000. My husband has to spend the rest of his life in pain. His only option for any real relief consists of 2 Hail Mary surgeries that could only give him a 50% positive rating. I was angry and devastated. Because of the actions of criminals, we were paying the price. For 18 years, my husband dutifully served our state, and for 14 years, our family sacrificed time, energy, and safety to live out his calling. In one night, it was all gone, as was any help. A handful of our friends were the only support we had as we navigated this new chapter of our lives while grieving the former one. We found ourselves back to square one, and I found myself growing angrier by the day. I would hear my husband scream in terror in his sleep as he dreamt of the nights of riots. I saw the devastation on his face because his career was gone in an instance. I felt betrayed by the very institution my husband took an oath to protect. No one was held accountable for his injury. No one got even so much as a ticket. No one saw the light; no one changed their ways. No one was suffering like we were. We did nothing wrong, yet we were the ones paying the consequences. While those who destroyed had millions of dollars thrown at them as they ascended to their hierarchy of wokism. For the first time in my life, my heart was hardening against the very people God called me to love.

I knew this was dangerous territory and my perspective was off, so I prayed for God to protect my heart. I began praying for our nation, but most of all, the Holy Spirit told me to pray for the rioters. The last thing I wanted to do was pray for them, but I have learned that when the Holy Spirit tells you to do something, it's better for you to be obedient. You see, it's easy to pray for those you love, but it's not so easy to pray for your enemies, at first. The more I prayed for them, the more my heart hurt for them. How heavy the burden of anger and hate must be in their hearts for them to lash out so violently? What had they seen and experienced in their lives to believe in something so wrong? I knew that without Christ in their hearts, they would spend forever apart from the eternal goodness of God. That broke me. I grieved for them, I prayed for them, and I began witnessing to them any chance I got. Not because I am great or perfect, but because Jesus is. He is the Redeemer, the Unifier, the One and Only Hope. That's the root of it all, isn't it? Without hope, fear takes hold.

Fear is the devil's playground, where he lies to us and deceives us into believing we can save ourselves or that hope doesn't exist. It easy to love your enemy when you don't have true enemies, and the reality is, most of us in America don't have enemies that disrupt our daily lives. It is exceptionally hard to truly love your enemies, so hard that you can't without Christ's grace and the Holy Spirit working on your heart daily. Satan wants to create discourse, he wants to divide us in hopes we will be ripe for the taking. He uses social media, the media, friends, celebrities, and even some pulpits to try and achieve his agenda. Don't let him. Immerse yourself in the Word of God, lean into the promises of our Father. Spend time talking to Jesus and being still for the Holy Spirit to talk to you. Let me tell you, friends, there is indeed hope; Jesus Christ is hope, hope for today, tomorrow, and eternity and forever more! We should love our enemies enough to tell them the good news and pray for them daily because Jesus loved us when we were enemies and Jesus alone can transform enemies into family in Christ!

We will always live with the trauma of the summer riots of 2020, as will most law enforcement families. Some businesses never recovered, some cities now lie broken and in ruins, and my husband will spend the rest of his life in pain… all because politics came to the streets of American cities in hopes of gaining power. But, God makes beauty of ashes, he restores even better than before. God has called our family into a new season. One where my husband's character, law enforcement expertise, and his heart for God and people will lead an office with God at the head. Above all, Jesus has taught us how to truly love our enemies, as we too were enemies when he gave his life in exchange for ours. We learned that even Christians can get it wrong sometimes, even with best of intentions but you can't judge God on the misguided actions of his children. We are all broken but Christ' church is one body, one family, and you don't leave family for differences of opinion. Any hardship or fiery trial that makes us more like Christ and less like our sinful selves… is worth ever ounce of heartache.

I don't know what the future holds but I know everything flows through God's hand and every fire we walk through is refining us like Silver so that we may be a reflection of Christ. I praise him for loving us enough to sanctify us, for walking with us through the fires….for Refined Silver.

Refined Silver

"I will bless the Lord at all times; his praise shall continually be in my mouth. My soul makes its boast in the Lord; let the humble hear and be glad. Oh, magnify the Lord with me, and let us exalt his name together! I sought the Lord, and he answered me and delivered me from all my fears."

Psalm 34:1-4

Refined Silver

~ Epilogue ~

If you made it this far, then you have read all about my darkest days. I know some were hard to read; they were even harder to live through. I could have glossed over them or made them more P.C., but I wanted to show you that true evil exists. That the world is broken and messy, and just how depraved we as humans are. When you see darkness as it truly is, Jesus brings everything into perspective. He brings hope and light to a lost and dying world. He turns destruction into a transformation far grander than what originally was. I hope you focused not on the fires I walked through, but on the redemption, protection, and triumph God provided every step of the way. Like Shadrach, Meshach, and Abednego, there was another in the fire with me!

The fact that the God of the Universe wanted me, a discarded orphan, and adopted me into his family wrecks me! Knowing what Jesus endured for my sake and yours wrecks me! The mere mention of Christ's sacrifice always brings me to tears. No matter how many times I have heard it, it always wrecks me. I was destined for hell on earth and eternity thereafter, but he loved me enough to rescue me, to save me from my sinful self. His love for me nailed his hands to the cross, and my sins nailed his feet to the wood. He took my shame and made it his own, and after all the torture, the beatings, and the mocking. He endured a slow, agonizing, and painful death for me... and you. When bad things happen in life, we as humans lose sight of God's love and often times we blame him as we lose perspective on His goodness. As Peter showed us, if you take your eyes off of Christ, you will sink. You will drown in your sorrows and go through life carrying the hurt and the heaviness of the trauma, allowing it to forever weigh you down.

Perspective changes everything. Your perspective of what is going on in the moment, in the situation, or in your life is filtered by the lens through which you see them. Everyone gets so caught up in seeing things the way they want to perceive them that they end up with a bad translation, aka a bad perspective. We view events through the lens of trauma, anger, pride, or resentment. The lens through which you view things determines how you see things. If I gave you a pair of dark-tinted sunglasses and asked you to describe the land and sky at night, everything would be dark, bland, and lonely. You would miss out on the stars, the silhouettes of the trees and the moon, which would be a small light without any spectacular attributes to it. But if I gave you a telescope, you would see the same land and sky but with a magical perspective. Insurmountable stars twinkling, the sheer brilliance and magical depths of the moon instead of just a circular light . The silhouettes of the trees come alive as you watch them sway to the lulling creatures singing their nightly lullaby. There are blessings in every situation. I challenge you to look back on some of your hardest times under a different set of lenses and you will find that while it might have been dark, there were more blessings that surrounded it that you didn't see at the time. Change your lens, look for the magic even in the dark, and watch your perspective change. Change your perspective when you are running late for work, hustling back and forth to extra-curricular activities, when your plans falling through, a toxic relationship ended, etc. You will see God even in the little things. After that, look back with your new lens, look back at your hard times. What are the positive things that surrounded or followed those dark times that you missed the first time?

Intentionally search for God in the hardest and darkest times. Open up his Word, his story, and write his words and his promises on your heart. God is omniscient; he knows all. God is omnipresent; he is with you in every situation through the end of time. He doesn't need a telescope. We, as mere humans, are bad about putting on our shades when it's dark and we begin to stumble around in fear and hopelessness of our nearsighted experiences in the dark. But if you change the lens to a telescope, it may still be dark, but it is surrounded by magical, breathtaking views and God's grace and mercy! Trusting God when your life is easy, when everyone is healthy, and finances are well, is easy to do. But, it's in the weary times that our faith grows, where God meets us in our brokenness, where Christ sustains us, and the intimacy with the Holy Spirit is bonded. It's in the hard times of life where our knees bow before God in earnest conviction, earnestly crying out to God for mercy. In the rawness of our pain, we are readily reminded that only Christ can save us and only God can provide purpose in the pain. It's those darkest moments of life where God refines us, where he strips us of our sinful and worldly flesh and he transforms us from the inside out . Because of my darkest times, I am better for it. With each season, God created a new me, each one a more completed image of Christ found in me. I don't know what you have experienced, but chances are, I've experienced something similar to how you are feeling and I can offer empathy and honestly tell you, Jesus restores even better.

Jesus knows trauma, far more than most, if any, of us ever will. Yet, knowing how it would end, he still took on flesh and came down to earth to save us. His love is limitless, and he offers your hope, love, and healing from your trauma. I am who I am today because God refined me. I am strong because I've known weakness. I am compassionate because I have experienced suffering. I laugh every chance I get because I have known true sadness. I love because I have known loss. I am a great mother because my children deserve the mother I needed growing up. I survived, healed and rebuilt stronger because Christ loved me too much to leave me there. I don't have all the answers, but I have learned a lot throughout my life. I end this book with some imparted words of wisdom:

Refined Silver

~ It is important to have Christian friends that encourage and cheer you on but also hold you accountable, coach you, and help you grow. If they don't tell you the truth out of love, they are "yes men," not friends.

~ Your home should be the antidote to stress, not the cause of it.

~Happiness is not a permanent state. Wholeness is, don't confuse the two. Only Christ and truly knowing yourself and loving yourself can bring wholeness.

~When all else fails, pray about it and take a nap. A lot of Jesus and a little extra sleep can change how we feel or at least our perspective.

~Get outside, sit in the sun, and take in God's creation.

~You have to know your worth before you can expect people to treat you as worthy.

~You have to love yourself. Only then can you give your love away and receive love in return.

~Self-care is crucial. You can't pour into others if you're an empty vessel yourself.

Refined Silver

~Pray without ceasing and then… pray some more.

~Everyone is fighting some sort of battle that you know nothing about. Be kind and offer grace and mercy.

~You can be weary or you can be a warrior. You can't be both.

~Even storms have their purpose.

~God is faithful. His track record is perfect. He has brought you through 100% of your hardest days. Don't doubt him now.

~Pain and suffering make for a better tomorrow. Jesus took on pain and suffering to save us. In the pain and suffering is where intimacy with Christ is nurtured. It gives purpose and it strengthens us. In our weakness, we turn to God, looking to him instead of ourselves.

~Life is short… eat the cake!

~Healthy boundaries are essential! If someone crosses those boundaries, let them know and give them the opportunity to rectify their behavior. Regardless, if they are family, church, or your friends, it's OK to remove

Refined Silver

them from your life until they are willing to respect those boundaries.

~In order to forgive, you must first sit with your grieve. Passing it over doesn't allow your heart to heal. Instead, the offense just clings to your heart, slowly hardening it against the person who wronged you. Afterwards, give it to God, give him time to heal your pain and depend on the Holy Spirit to change your broken heart to a forgiving one. Forgive and let go. If you hold onto the wrong, you didn't truly forgive.

~The Word of God is alive; it breathes, cuts, restores, and It provides solace. It isn't an ancient document, it's God's story of the fall, search, and rescue of you and I through Christ. Sit with it daily, mediate over it, pray over it. Write the words of God on your heart.

~God created you to be you. It's OK if you're a Peter and not a Paul. Don't let the world tell you that you are different than who God says you are. I don't fit in with most people and that's OK, because God has called me onto a different path. Your path is different too.

~ Everyone cannot go where God calls you to go, you will outgrow some people, and that is OK. Give them and you the grace to move on without hard feelings.

Refined Silver

~Always tell your friends and family that you love them, because you may not be able to tomorrow.

~ Don't let a bad day make you feel like you have a bad life.

~Masculinity isn't toxic! The absence of it is! The world needs more masculine godly men, not less. They are protectors, leaders, and loving. Men without masculinity are weak, unguided, abusive, and spiteful.

~ Integrity is everything. It's who you are when others aren't looking.

~Unapologetically love with all your heart. Go out of your way to help others. I've never regretted helping someone, but I have regretted not helping many times.

~Make sure the perception of yourself and how others perceive you match up. If not, you have work to do.

~Be Bold yet Kind…life is too short to be a lesser version of yourself or to walk on eggshells.

~Be obsessively grateful for what God has given you. From a pair of white socks to a million dollar house. They are all gifts from God!

~ Read anything and everything. There is real world magic in books!

~ You're never too old to believe in fairy tales, magic, love, and Santa Claus. This broken world is hard enough; cling onto any magic or innocence you can. And for the love of all that is good, stop forcing your kids to stop believing in these things. They have 18 years before the realities of the world hit them… Let children be children for as long as they can!

~Be a background leader. Help others, take charge, do good, but do it in a way that God gets the glory… not you!

~Laughter is important, but so is an occasional good cry. Don't miss out on a life of one for other.

~Choose your spouse wisely, because you are choosing the parent of your children, your forever best friend, and the one who will be holding your hand on your death bed. Marriage is sacred, instituted by God alone. The relationship between a husband and a wife is far more than a piece of paper. Stop treating marriage with an escape clause… it's for life!

~ Outside of God, nothing should come before or between your spouse, you and your children as long as it aligns with God and is a healthy relationship. Protect that sanctuary and do not let others interfere.

~ Try everything(legal and Godly) at least once. How will you know what you love if you never get out of your comfort zone? You won't!

~ Get your annual check-ups!! Women and men included. An annual check-up can save your life!

~ You know your body more than anyone. You know your children more than anyone. You are your own and their own advocate! Do not let others steal your voice, regardless of their position or how many initials that follow their name.

~Above all else, surrender to Jesus! He loves you!! He wants all of you, the broken, the lost, the hurt. Nothing you have ever done is too terrible for Jesus to forgive!

Made in the USA
Columbia, SC
06 January 2023